G R JORDAN

A Time to Rest

AHighlands and Islands Detective Thriller #38

In many walks of life, a conscience is
a more expensive encumbrance than
a wife or a carriage.

Thomas de Quincey

Contents

Foreword

The events of this book, while based around real and also fictitious locations around Scotland and England, are entirely fictional and all characters do not represent any living or deceased person. All companies are fictitious representations. This book should be read in a gold leaf carriage of unknown origin.

Acknowledgments

To Ken, Jean, Colin, Evelyn, John and Rosemary for your work in bringing this novel to completion, your time and effort is deeply appreciated.

Books by G R Jordan

The Highlands and Islands Detective series (Crime)

1. Water's Edge
2. The Bothy
3. The Horror Weekend
4. The Small Ferry
5. Dead at Third Man
6. The Pirate Club
7. A Personal Agenda
8. A Just Punishment
9. The Numerous Deaths of Santa Claus
10. Our Gated Community
11. The Satchel
12. Culhwch Alpha
13. Fair Market Value
14. The Coach Bomber
15. The Culling at Singing Sands
16. Where Justice Fails
17. The Cortado Club
18. Cleared to Die
19. Man Overboard!
20. Antisocial Behaviour
21. Rogues' Gallery
22. The Death of Macleod - Inferno Book 1

23. A Common Man - Inferno Book 2
24. A Sweeping Darkness - Inferno Book 3
25. Dormie 5
26. The First Minister - Past Mistakes Book 1
27. The Guilty Parties - Past Mistakes Book 2
28. Vengeance is Mine - Past Mistakes Book 3
29. Winter Slay Bells
30. Macleod's Cruise
31. Scrambled Eggs
32. The Esoteric Tear
33. A Rock 'n' Roll Murder
34. The Slaughterhouse
35. Boomtown
36. The Absent Sculptor
37. A Trip to Rome
38. A Time to Rest
39. Cinderella's Carriage
40. Wild Swimming

Kirsten Stewart Thrillers (Thriller)

1. A Shot at Democracy
2. The Hunted Child
3. The Express Wishes of Mr MacIver
4. The Nationalist Express
5. The Hunt for 'Red Anna'
6. The Execution of Celebrity
7. The Man Everyone Wanted
8. Busman's Holiday

The Patrick Smythe Series (Crime)

1. The Disappearance of Russell Hadleigh
2. The Graves of Calgary Bay
3. The Fairy Pools Gathering

Austerley & Kirkgordon Series (Fantasy)

1. Crescendo!
2. The Darkness at Dillingham
3. Dagon's Revenge
4. Ship of Doom

Supernatural and Elder Threat Assessment Agency (SETAA) Series (Fantasy)

1. Scarlett O'Meara: Beastmaster

Island Adventures Series (Cosy Fantasy Adventure)

1. Surface Tensions

Dark Wen Series (Horror Fantasy)

1. The Blasphemous Welcome
2. The Demon's Chalice

Chapter 01

Alan Macmillan had seen a lot of changes in his life. Some for the better. He wasn't one of these people who got stuck in the past, wishing for the better times, wishing for when things were simpler. For instance, getting to the quayside, Alan liked how he had a car which heated quickly and his windscreen cleared almost instantly. He drove in comfort. Yes, it wasn't the most up to date, but it got him about, and when push came to shove, how far could you really drive on the islands?

Alan lowered the last of his pots onto the boat and prepared to untie from the quay. This was a joy, one that had changed little over the years. Totter around in a small boat and drop his pots, and then go back out to check them another day. He had some already down and once he dropped these in, he would have a look for the harvest.

The Isle of Harris had been his home for years and he had never thought about going away. Then, in his late thirties, when he'd met Morag, he decided he definitely wasn't going away. She was a younger woman, maybe ten years or so, but she was ready to set up home, as was he. However, in one of those unkind blows of life, she'd been unable to have children, or rather, they had been unable.

Some of the family always seemed to blame her, but it took two to tango, as they say. Alan wasn't sure if it was him or it was her. Well, they were fairly sure it wasn't him; he had never got checked, not properly. They'd just sort of given up on the idea.

But that was fine, because they had each other, and they had their life. And it was a happy one. She tended to the croft. He fished. They had their friends, and they had their annual holiday. Two weeks in the sun. Not really Alan's cup of tea, but he went for Morag; after all, she deserved it. She worked hard for him, hard for their life, and she patiently waited for her time in the sun.

It wasn't that sunny today, on the east side of Harris, but it wasn't too bad either. The sea, after what had been a rough night, was much calmer, and as he got onto his boat, he found it was more than adequate for sea legs.

Alan took in a deep breath of air. That's what he liked here— that freshness. He turned on the engine, scanned around him, making sure he was clear of everything, and tottered out on the boat, down the small loch. His eventual destination would be Loch Ghreosabhagh, where he had pots to check. But here, closer to Stockinish, he would drop some of his own. As he rounded the spit of land at the end of the bay, he could see it. The one thing he wasn't too happy about on this beloved isle of his.

Recently, tourism numbers had gone up. Everyone wanted to come out to the Hebrides. Everyone wanted to get their own piece of a holiday. There had been all the fighting over the campervans.

One of them had stopped in a car park that was next to the

local burial ground. That was unwise, as the campervan was still there when a funeral turned up. Some islanders didn't react to tourism hospitably. But neither did some tourists treat the place with respect.

Alan was one of those people who could see both sides of the argument. He wished the extremes would just shut up, and let those in the middle come to an amicable agreement. Some of his friends had done all right out of the tourism. They had full B&Bs, trips out to see dolphins, or other features of the wildlife, while others had resented it greatly.

Come out here in their camper vans. They buy all their food on the mainland and jump on the boat.

The boat. Now that was something. The ferry situation across to the islands had always caused consternation to some degree, but now in the summer it was getting crazy. Trying to book passage off the island in your car was next to impossible. The tourists filled it up.

Some people on the island travelled back and forward regularly. It was a lifeline service, as they said. Alan was one of those people who said that spots should be kept for a certain number of islanders a day. But it hadn't happened and the arguments and debates went on. He got away from those things out here with a sea breeze in his hair and the joy of a sea-borne life.

However, he cursed the building he looked at now, located on the far side of the loch. Multi-million-pound resort is what they'd said. Not that big, to be honest. But there was a lot of money in that spa resort. And those who came to it were not tourists.

They were big names. People with serious money. There were a couple of locals who had got jobs in there, doing many of the menial tasks, but they brought in specialists, as they put it, to treat the clients. All to get yourself put in some sort of water. Alan looked about the boat. What's wrong with the water around here?

Spa treatments? Apparently, they put you in seaweed. They distilled brews of something or other from the local area. Everything was natural. Out here on his boat, he caught a whiff of the diesel. Maybe not everything was perfect, but he wasn't going to . . . he didn't know. He gave a sigh and attended to his pots as he went up the sea loch.

There was the odd car that passed by along what they called the Golden Road. Well, it wasn't actually a Golden Road, was it? It was the road that ran round the edge of the east of Harris. It dipped up and down and usually caused havoc with tourists. They went too quick over the dips that then turned hard right, almost putting their cars into ditches or off the edge. And then they got stuck looking at each other because they didn't know how to use passing places on the roadside.

It made Alan laugh. And not in a nasty way. But there were more and more cars coming down this way. More and more of the tranquillity ripped apart. He couldn't quite say that of the spa.

The place kept itself to itself. In fact, he didn't really know anybody in it. A couple of women who cleaned, he knew from the village. But really, they were just doing offices and that. They weren't dealing with any of the big money parts of the spa.

Alan went further up the loch and was soon approaching his last pot. His shoulders were aching now. It was rough work, and he wasn't getting any younger. Still, it wouldn't be long before he turned and headed back to where Morag would have the kettle on. Tonight was going to be a quiet night in with her. When he headed back for lunch, she would begin with a smile. Life was sweet. The two of them had found their spot, here in the undisturbed—or at least mainly undisturbed—side of Harris. This was home. Right here!

Alan went back to his small wheelhouse and was ready to turn the boat around when he looked across at the shore. Just down from the road, he could see something. He thought it was green; at least in the morning's light, that's what it looked like. When he had started out, the day was darker. But now, the sun was as high as it really tended to get on a November day. Though his stomach was churning from hunger, and he was ready to head back round to his own loch, he couldn't just leave. This wasn't right.

Sometimes you got bits of debris lying along the shore. But this detritus didn't seem to be something that could have got to its location except from above. Alan went closer in the boat until he was worried that he was so close in that the bottom of the boat might scrape against rock. He dropped an anchor, and got his tiny boat, a little rubber dinghy, and climbed into the back of it.

His interest was piqued by this green thing. It was probably about the length of a man, and actually, thought Alan, about the width of a man from what he could see. He'd have to clamber over a few rocks to get a look at it, but he would do.

He brought the dinghy alongside and pulled it up onto some rocks. It'd be okay there. It wouldn't drift off. He clambered across the rocks, watching, careful in case his feet would slip. These rocks were not the kindest, and if you fell over, you could easily cut yourself, never mind take an enormous bang to the shoulder, or worse, to the leg. He also wasn't somewhere

where you could easily shout for help.

Alan made his way slowly along, looking for a less steep route to where the object was. As he approached it, he realised that it was seaweed. Plenty of seaweed, but almost like the seaweed was bundling something.

He reached out with his hand, and yes, it was moist, still slippery. But then again, it had been wet last night, hadn't it? Proper dreich. The sun hadn't been too warm this morning, either.

Around the coast, there was a damp atmosphere, especially now that it was November. It wasn't like summer when things would dry on the rocks quickly. He reached down, touched the seaweed, then prodded it. Well, there wasn't something easily collapsible inside. He felt some resistance.

Alan stood up slightly. It really was about the size of a human, wasn't it? He reached forward to see if he could lift some of the seaweed off. Carefully, he peeled it back.

He reeled. That looked like flesh. It was white. Looked cold. But it looked like flesh. Alan stood for a moment, unsure what to do. He looked around. There wasn't anybody. Should he shout for help? Should he go back and call people? But what if they all came in and, well . . .

What if this was something else? Maybe he'd got it wrong, and it wasn't flesh. Maybe it was just something that looked similar.

Alan looked around. He moved his hands up the outside of the object. *Could those be shoulders?* he wondered. He thought about checking, but his body seemed to be paralysed. In one sense, his mind was running in a rational state, trying to work out what was going on. Was this a person? And another part of his mind was reeling, his muscles involuntarily refusing to move.

Come on, he said to himself. *Otherwise, she'll be laughing her head off at me when I get back. Or be angry.*

Morag wouldn't be impressed if he just walked away from this. She'd always been a woman who did the right thing, no matter how difficult that was. He remembered how she had cared for a neighbour who was falling apart. Broken parts of the bodily functions. He remembered the bed, the urine, and more that she'd dealt with and cleaned up, when frankly, he didn't want to go near it. *Come on*, he said to himself.

Alan crept round a little further, moving up to what he considered to be the top end of the figure. *It is a figure*, he thought. *It looks like a figure.* He reached to where a head would be, except it seemed bloated.

He pulled at the seaweed around the figure, reaching forward now with two hands, pushing it back. *It's getting thin.* He pushed again, and this time an eye looked back at him.

Alan reeled backwards, took a step with his right foot, missed the rock behind, and tumbled to his right. His hands shot out, grabbing a slippery rock, but what he landed on dug into his side. He let out a yell and then forced himself to scramble to get back into a stable position. As he did so, his heart was pounding.

That was an eye. That's a person. That's a . . .

He crawled forward again. This time, he looked at the eye. It wasn't looking back at him, but the eyelid was fixed open, and the eye was staring, with no life, up towards the cloudy sky. Alan reached forward, and against all better judgement, pulled away the seaweed around the face. He breathed a sigh of relief. It was no one he knew.

Then he chastised himself. *This was somebody, and they were dead. How can I feel like that?*

For a moment, clarity came to Alan's mind. He was standing on rocks, unable to contact anyone, looking at a body wrapped in seaweed. *What on earth?* he thought. *Seaweed?*

He looked over towards the spa resort. *They were the ones who used the seaweed. Did this go wrong? Did they just dump somebody? Should I take the body?*

He reached down, looking at the face. And this time, he slapped it. Alan wasn't sure why. The body did nothing. Unrelenting, the eye kept looking up at the sky. The other one was closed. Alan shivered. *What to do?*

He turned and walked back to his dinghy, wanting to put distance between himself and the body. Placing the dinghy back in the water, he got in and rowed his way back over to his own boat. Once there, he put the dinghy back into the boat, rather than leaving it tied to the side. *Because I'm not getting back in there. I'm not going over to look at that body again.*

Alan started the boat up and took it out of the loch, just along the side of the coast. There was a large aerial up here. He could contact the Coastguard. The mobile signal was often dodgy, and he didn't want to contact the police. The Coastguard could do that.

He had never really talked to the police. Whereas he had in his life talked to the Coastguard. Alan picked up the handset on the radio and made his call. He certainly wasn't going back over to where that body was again.

Chapter 02

Hope McGrath stood inside the door of the glamping pod, looking out. The view wasn't terrific, but where this glamping pod was situated was very private. So private that she was standing at the door, uncovered, and quite happy about it. There was no one within miles.

Behind her on the bed lay John, her partner. He was asleep, and rightly too, despite the later time of the morning. He hadn't got a lot of sleep last night, and as she stood looking out, Hope was content in one way, but also a little anxious.

She was on call today and could be summoned at any moment. She'd worked hard to find this glamping pod. The mobile reception was good, so she could be reached at any point. And yet, it was so far away. She was alone with John.

She reached down and touched her bare belly. This would have to work, she thought. These times, enjoyable as they were, needed to end. She didn't quite understand it. There was a loneliness within her despite being with John. A hunger, a desire. It had come like the turning on of a switch. Never in her life had Hope wanted kids, until recently. But then again, she'd never been as settled as she was now with John. Her car man. It wasn't glamorous. But he was solid.

What sort of word was that? she thought. *Solid. Dependable. Always there. Always!*

She turned and looked at him, sprawled on the bed with a sheet covering his midriff. He was fantastic. She smiled. He'd make a great dad, too. She'd seen him with small kids, whenever he'd had the chance to interact with them. And the one thing about John was, he was undaunted by them. Hope couldn't say the same, and yet she wanted one of her own.

She turned back to look out. Life was funny. She stood there for a moment and then heard a sound behind her. She didn't turn, as feet padded towards her. Two arms slipped around her waist, and she felt a kiss on her neck.

'I would like to advise you that standing starkers at a door, visible to all and sundry who come by, is not the behaviour of a detective inspector,' said John, teasing her.

'No?'

A blanket was wrapped around her. His arms curled over the blanket, pulling her close. 'You didn't need to do that,' she said.

'Yes, I did,' said John. 'Look at you, you're standing at a glass door. It's glass, you can see everything from outside.'

Hope thought about when she was younger. Macleod would have called her hedonistic back then. And yes, there's been a wild streak in her. Maybe this was her rebelling back to those times. She was a mix of emotions, she knew that, a hunger for a little one in her life and yet not wanting to become one of those types of mums.

She was still the detective inspector. She'd worked hard to get to the rank. Macleod was giving her more and more free rein. He trusted her. Hope was running the investigations, a lot of them anyway. His move up had been one that had shocked her, because Hope had thought Macleod would never leave that rank. And maybe he'd done it for her. That was the thing about Seoras; there was a kind heart underneath a grumpy exterior.

'You think it'll work this time?' asked Hope.

'How would I know?' said John. 'I'm just happy to keep on trying.'

She gave a giggle. She was sure he would be. That was men for you. Not that she was not enjoying herself. She was as happy in his company as she'd ever been in anyone's.

'We don't have to do anything,' said Hope. 'We can just spend the rest of the day here. An entire weekend—'

Her mobile vibrated on the counter across from her.

'No, no, no!' she said, out loud, and turned to march over towards the phone, slipping out of John's arms. The blanket somehow remained vaguely intact as she picked up the phone until she sat down on the bed, where the blanket fell away completely.

'Perry, I really hope this is important.'

'No,' said Perry, 'I thought I'd phone you on your day off, when you've mysteriously disappeared out of sight and sound, just for a giggle.'

'What is it?' asked Hope.

'I'm sorry to interrupt,' he said, 'but they've found a body on the Isle of Harris.'

'Right,' said Hope. 'What do you mean "a body?"'

'Off the side of the road, down towards the sea, on some rocks.'

'Suspicious?'

'Well, they've been out to look at it, and cornered it off for us.'

'You can get yourself over, can't you?' prompted Hope. 'You can take this one, Perry, can't you? For me?'

'I would do,' said Perry. 'But I think it's going to be more than a one-person job.'

'We not got anyone else?'

'No. Susan went off, didn't she, to get her leg sorted? Ross has got that thing with his kid you didn't want to pull him away from. And he's not on call. You are. So, I had to go to you first.'

'Okay, Perry,' said Hope. 'You did right. Maybe you can head over, and I'll join you soon.'

'No,' said Perry, 'I'm afraid not. It's requiring you.'

'It's a body and some rocks,' said Hope. 'I get it, I'll need to come over, but you can do the initial. You can get over and—'

'No,' said Perry. 'I'm afraid it's going to be one of those jobs.'

'Those jobs?'

'Yeah. Looks like there's some important people in the middle of this. It's a big posh spa or something. Local guys are struggling. I'm struggling with them. I need some clout.'

'What sort of spa?'

'Well, I did a quick internet search, and it was built not that long ago. Year or two. It seems, however, that people who really are people go there. Movie stars, boxers, people in the public eye. One of these health-fad things.'

'Well, you book the flights then.'

'I will do,' said Perry. 'Also, that if I just went, well, you're talking health-fad people. They might not react that well to me. You look the part a lot more than me.'

'Don't put yourself down,' said Hope. 'After all, you've quit the ciggies.'

'And a lot of good that's doing me,' said Perry. 'Anyway, I'll get these flights booked.'

Hope closed the call and sat for a moment, thinking. 'Fat lot of good that's doing me,' Perry had said. He hadn't taken well to the fact that Susan was keeping him on the edge. DC Susan Cunningham was getting a prosthetic fitted for her leg. And would be out of the equation for a while.

It had left Hope with DC Perry and DS Ross, both of whom were excellent officers. But Perry was right. If this involved TV stars or people who were high up in the public sphere, Hope would need to be there? *Blast it*, she thought.

She was suddenly aware that John was on his knees in front of her, looking up into her face. She was so focused, she'd completely forgot about him.

'You got to go?' he whispered.

'I got to go. Harris as well. Not even local.'

'It's okay,' he said. 'We have given it a go.' She reached forward with her hands, reaching for his and holding them tight.

'I'm sorry,' she said. 'This seems to be the thing that's driving me at the moment. Every time we have time off, I just want to, well, you know, I just—'

'it's not a chore,' said John suddenly. 'You know, it's not something that I'm struggling with being part of.' He gave a laugh. 'I'm more worried about you. If things don't work out quickly, if things don't happen soon, if—'

'I know. I . . . well—' The phone rang again. She reached over. Hope smiled and then answered it.

'Seoras,' she said, looking at the face on the phone. Macleod wasn't exactly beaming back at her, but getting Macleod to smile in a photograph was one of the hardest things to do in life.

'Sorry to disturb you,' he said, 'but—'

'Perry's already been on to me.'

'Well, you'd better think about getting on the move,' said Macleod. 'The Tides of Tranquillity Spa Resort.'

'I've never heard of it,' she said.

'Multi-million-pound spa resort,' said Macleod. 'Plonked onto the Isle of Harris. Over on the east side of the moon.'

'The what?'

'The moon. We were down there, if you remember. Not long after we started working together. We followed that killer all the way down to Harris. Ended up on a boat. It was a nasty one. She could have ended both of us. But she didn't.'

'That was the scandal of the trafficked women,' said Hope. 'Down near that.'

'Just up from it. Some saw it as a fantastic way to promote the benefits of the island. All the good things. Nature, wildlife, seaweed. Well, this one's going to be a cracker,' he said, 'because the body's been found wrapped up in seaweed.'

'And you're going to tell me they wrap people up in seaweed at the resort.'

'I am, and I do not have a clue why people would want to do that. Cold seaweed. Ridiculous,' said Macleod, 'but apparently people who are quite famous like to have it done to them, as well as a lot of other crazy things. So, how are you getting down there?'

'Perry's sorting out the flights. I'll get there as quick as I can.'

'You far from home at the moment?' asked Macleod,

'Close enough,' she said,

'Sorry to disturb,' he said, 'but I'm getting a lot of heat. I'm going to follow you down. I'll bring Ross, if you want him as well.'

'Of course, we'll want Ross.'

'Good. There are a few things here to deal with and also if I'm up here,' said Macleod, 'I can keep the top brass away from you. What we don't want is a circus going on out there. Harris is a small place.'

'Do you know who's there at the resort—who this could be?' asked Hope.

'It's not one of the guests,' said Macleod. 'If it was, that would have leaked by now. That would be out. We've got no confirmation, but I think it's one of the workers.'

'Great,' said Hope. 'It might be easier if it had been one of the famous people. Just some lunatic killing them.'

'Get down, Find out what's going on. I'll be about.'

Hope put down the phone and turned to look at John. 'We'd better get going, unless you want to stay?'

'We're in a glamping pod in the back end of nowhere, or at least well hidden from everyone, so why would I want to stay here without you?'

She smiled and watched as he went to get the clothes out of the bag they hadn't even unpacked. Hope walked forward again and stood at the door. She put her hands down to her belly.

Something. She wasn't sure, but something felt different. It was hard to explain, but something felt different. Something said to her that maybe this time it had worked. Something was . . .

She felt a blanket being wrapped around her again. 'I thought we just talked about this.' Hope shrugged the blanket off. She took John's hands and put them round her belly. 'I think something may have happened this time,' she said.

'How can you know that?' he asked. 'I mean, I thought you

had to do those tests and stuff to check and . . .'

'I don't know,' she said. 'Something just feels different. Something . . . I don't know.' She turned round and hugged him. 'I really hope so, John.'

He hugged her back. 'Get some clothes on. We need to get you away,' he said. Hope nodded, a slight tear emerging from her eye.

Chapter 03

Hope had made good time, and Perry had flown over to Stornoway with her to pick up a hire car and drive down to Harris. It wasn't long to get there compared to driving on the mainland distances. But the flight had been later on in the day, and so they were arriving in darkness by the time they got down.

From Stornoway, they took the road to Harris that wound past the Clisham, Perry narrowly avoiding a couple of sheep that were wandering round the road. Having been here before, Hope was well aware of this risk. They passed through Tarbert, and then headed down towards Leverburgh.

Macleod had been right. They had worked down here before, and it had been a case that almost saw their demise at the end. She hadn't known Seoras that well then, but the memories came back to her. Following the road round the east side of Harris, Perry coped admirably with the strange turns and twists until they got down to Loch Ghreosabhagh. There was a sign, splendidly massive, showing where the spa resort was. The Tides of Tranquillity.

'You'd have thought they would have put it in Gaelic,' said Perry, as he went to turn in.

'Why?' asked Hope.

'Fit in with the place. Everywhere has names which are Gaelic. Look at the guest houses, Ceol na Mara, you know, sounds of the sea. Things like that,' said Perry. 'Help endear them to the locals a bit more.'

'And the money they'll put into the economy, that wouldn't help?' said Hope.

'What money into the economy? I'm sure they've had to build it here, but you find out how many of the local companies got a part of that. Some of this stuff in here is very specialised. It wouldn't be on the islands.'

'But you still have to run it, you still have food, you still have—'

'Hope,' said Perry, 'the people in here, they're not C-list celebs, they're not sitting here on the back end of Radio Scotland or BBC Alba. These are the people who are A-listers. A lot of them, they're paying crazy money,'

Hope hadn't had much of a chance to look and see what was going on regarding the spa resort. Perry, however, seemed to have done a lot of his homework.

'Well then,' said Hope, 'something to keep in mind, in case there's a fracture between the locals and those running it. That would be a good reason for murder.'

'It would be, but it's very extreme,' said Perry. 'Places like this, there are always problems, aren't there, when you modernise and you bring things in from elsewhere. Some people see it as interfering; some people see progress. You don't see murder with it, though.'

Hope nodded. Perry pulled the car up alongside a young constable. With Perry's badge in the window, they were waved through. As Hope exited the car, a uniformed sergeant approached her.

'Detective Inspector. I'm sorry. Sergeant Peter McNeil.' The man was in his late fifties, by the look of it, and certainly had the island accent. It was often in the force over in the islands that you got people who weren't local. Many did a couple of years on the teams before heading back off to other posts. But there were some who stayed and stayed for good. Or were from here and came back. McNeil seemed to be one of them.

'Nasty business,' said McNeil.

'Well, Peter, this is Detective Constable Perry. He just gets Perry. Doesn't like anyone to call him anything else.'

'I know my place,' said Perry with a smile. 'What have you got for us?'

'The body's down towards the loch. Further down. They're there at the moment. Forensics have only just got here. They've done well to get across so quick. I'm sure they'll give you a little more detail. We believe the victim could be an Oswaldo Hernandez.'

'The DCI said it wasn't a guest,' said Hope.

'Mr Hernandez is not a guest. He works here. An Argentinian by birth, now a Swiss national working long-term on a visa. The Spa manager should be able to fill you in more details about just exactly who he is. She's inside. I'll take you to meet her first.'

'Thank you,' said Hope and followed Peter McNeil inside, accompanied by Perry.

From the outside, the centre looked impressive. It was modern, with many glass windows. Obviously there for the guests to appreciate the scenery around as you couldn't see in. Now Hope remembered Harris. It was, as Macleod had put it, like the moon. Plenty of rock formation around, but here in the darkness, none of it could be seen. The night was overcast, and Hope was struggling to see beyond the lit grounds of the spa resort.

Once inside, the interior took on what Hope could only describe as a high-quality medical facility. Everything was clean and crisp. Yet it was quite sterile, not friendly, not warm, but maybe that wasn't the point. Maybe the point was to look clinical, to encourage those coming to feel that they were getting treatment, not simply having a holiday.

From behind a white counter, a woman approached. She was only slightly smaller than Hope, and had a very erect stance. Maybe she's one of the movie stars, Hope thought, for she had long blonde hair running down in waves onto her shoulders. The woman was dressed in a neat black skirt that hugged her hips, and she had a smile that could have been used for an advert. Adorned in a crisp white blouse which was certainly not vulgar, she displayed a small pendant around her neck.

Hope thought she looked like one of those women that men believed should be their secretary. Professional looking, and yet with an obvious allure. Hope wondered if she had the same issues that Hope did—being looked at, less for her abilities, and more for her appearance.

'Detective Inspector, this is Maddy Lyle. She's the spa manager. Miss Lyle, this is Detective Inspector Hope McGrath.'

'I'm delighted to meet you, Detective Inspector. Obviously, not delighted by the circumstances.'

'But, of course,' said Hope.

'Let's see if we can get this tidied up quickly,' said Maddy.

'We'll get this tidied up as quickly as we can. And, quite frankly, I don't like the word tidied up,' said Hope, 'with regards to an investigation. We have someone who's died, possibly in very dubious circumstances. If I have a murderer on the loose, I want to find them and find them quickly. But we will not be tidying up.'

'I didn't want to insinuate that,' said Maddy. 'I was just saying that I'm hoping we can keep this fairly quiet. The guests we have here, they come not looking to cause a fuss. Here they're away from everything and most of them have an issue that they're trying to deal with. We help with that. This is not a holiday resort; we are a clinical foundation.'

'I won't be publicising things any more than I have to,' said Hope. 'I would like from you a full list of who's staying at the resort. And we want to be speaking to the staff and guests in a few hours. First, I want to get out to the site where the body has been found. When I've done that, I'll be back. I appreciate it will be a late hour, but if you can keep people here.'

'Our guests have nowhere else to go.'

'I was talking about the staff. Do you have many who are local?' asked Hope.

'A few, but most of our specialists are from elsewhere, such as Oswaldo. We offer the very best in care. So—'

'That's great,' said Hope, quickly. 'Get me those lists, please, and plan for rooms where I can talk to people in private. If you'd be so good to do that and I'll get the sergeant here to make sure that we're not disturbed.'

'I fully expect the press to arrive,' said Maddy. 'My guests are well known, even if it's not known that they're here.'

'But things get out,' said Hope, 'especially when there's been a murder, if indeed that's what's happened.'

'I take it, this is not your first rodeo?' asked Maddy.

Hope stopped for a moment. Was the woman baiting her? Was she trying to dominate the conversation after Hope had put her back in her place?

'I'll be being joined as well by Detective Chief Inspector Macleod. That's mainly in case we get the press. He deals with that side. I'll be finding our murderer, if indeed we have one,' said Hope. 'If you have questions in the meantime, Detective Perry will give you his contact details, or you can speak to the sergeant. Both can reach me. For the meantime, thank you for your help and if you'd organise what I've asked for, I would be most grateful.'

Hope didn't give the woman a chance to respond and turned away. Maddy was clearly someone used to running her own show. Hope had dealt with people like this before and knew she'd have to keep an eye on her.

'I'm going to head out and see what's going on with the murder site,' she said to McNeil. 'I'll head down with Perry, okay? You stay here. First sign of a large contingent of press, let me know. Keep things as tight as you can, Peter. You may not be used to this sort of scrutiny, but just keep things tight.

'We'll be getting Sergeant Ross and DCI Macleod over soon. There'll be more of us to give you a hand. If you need numbers, say so. Macleod's got a lot of swing.'

'Of course, Hope,' said Peter.

Perry drove Hope down to the loch-side, parking the car where he could see the forensic van. As they approached it, one of the forensic officers waved them over and handed them some coveralls.

'The boss said you'd be on your way. Jona said to get these on. We've hardly touched the site at all.'

Hope changed, along with Perry, and climbed down a few rocks to where she saw a cordoned-off area.'

'Don't come in yet,' said a voice. She looked over and saw

blinding lights beaming down on a diminutive Asian woman.

'You all right?' asked Hope.

'Can we get our bodies in much more accessible places next time, please?' said Jona. 'Do you know what it's like trying to run power out here? We've got a generator going, and it's still a nightmare.'

'Can I get a—?'

'Sure,' said Jona. 'I'll just drop everything. I said, "Give me a minute."'

Hope gave a smile. She wouldn't have accepted that from anybody on the uniform side. But Jona was good at her job, and she was also a close friend. Approximately three minutes later, she approached Hope.

'Come on, then,' she said, 'down here. Watch your footing. It's slippery. I think we've got the photographs done, at least.'

She clambered down over rocks, Hope following, and Perry struggling a bit more. Soon they were close to where a body was wrapped up in seaweed.

'I've dug out an ID badge from the spa. This is Oswaldo Hernandez, according to the badge. The photograph fits the face, so I believe it is him.'

'That's who's missing,' said Hope. 'Argentinian man.'

'Well, he looks more European to me.'

'A Swiss National,' said Perry from behind Hope.

'Oh, speak to Ross about this. We need to get everything about this guy. Ross needs to go come through on that.'

'On it,' said Perry.

'What can you tell me so far?' asked Hope.

'It's a bit of a guesstimate at the moment, okay? So, by the looks of it, he's been killed and then wrapped in the seaweed. There's no puncture in the seaweed to say he was stabbed or attacked after he was wrapped up in it.'

'Is it a good job they've done with the seaweed,' asked Hope.

'In what way?' asked Jona.

'I mean, is this how they wrap people up? When they do it in the centre?'

'I have no idea,' said Jona. 'I'm a forensic officer. I'm not a spa treatments expert.'

'Are you all right?' said Hope. 'You're tetchy on it.'

Perry coughed, obviously not completely comfortable with the display that was going on.

'No,' said Jona. 'I'm not. It was a long night last night. And, well, forget it,' she said.

'What do you mean, "forget it?"'

Jona looked up at Perry. 'Girl talk. It'll be girl talk, okay? He doesn't need to know.'

'I can give you a moment,' said Perry.

'No,' said Jona. 'It's not important.'

'Tell me who he is, and I'll sort him,' said Perry.

Jona looked at Perry, startled, and Hope nearly burst out laughing. 'I never—'

'No, you didn't,' said Perry. 'But in fairness, recently you started going out a bit more in the evening, and it hasn't worked out for you. I can tell that from your face, your expression. Girl talk, so it's obviously something he's done that you will not talk to me about, which is fair enough. And h—'

Hope put her hand up to Perry. 'I think we've displayed your brilliance enough for today,' said Hope. 'It'll be girl talk.' Perry gave a nod and his face returned to a passive image, as if it never looked any other way.

'They wrapped him up in the seaweed,' said Jona. 'And he's

been dumped from up above on the roadside. I can't see a lot of car tracks. The car probably didn't go off the road. You could stop it here and there'd be nobody about. It'd be so easy. I mean, this is the back end of nowhere. Even for the Western Isles.'

'Update me when you can,' said Hope.

'I'll be working out of Stornoway, up in the Western Isles Hospital, the morgue up there. I have got nowhere to work from here. We're at the far end of this bit of civilisation,' said Jona.

Hope was only too well aware. She'd worked in far-off places too many times to not be aware of the issues that they raised.

'Right then, are you sure the body couldn't have got here from the sea.'

'That body has not been in the sea, it's been trapped in seaweed.'

'Could they have brought it to here on a boat?'

'Yes, but my goodness, that would be tough,' said Jona. 'Coming in there and trying to carry a body up there and dump it? You'd have to ask, why? I think they've tried to dump it from up there by the road, and then they've run and not realised it hasn't gone into the sea.'

'Why wrap it up in the seaweed, though?' asked Hope.

'To frame someone. To have kept it somewhere,' said Perry. 'If somebody's wrapped up in seaweed, you're not going to disturb them, are you?'

'Well, that's a point,' said Hope.

'I can't tell you much more at the moment,' said Jona. 'Might find more in daylight, maybe. We'll see about that. I'll get on to the work on the body up at the morgue.'

'Very good and we'll have a coffee and a chat when you're

ready for it.'

'He's nowhere near us when we do that, okay?' Jona said, pointing at Perry, but she was smiling.

As they climbed back up, took off their coverall suits and went back to the car, Hope thought about Perry. He had a warming influence now on the team in stark contrast to when he arrived. He had said at the time he was trying to fit in with what he thought was a more brusque crowd, remembering what Macleod's team had been like in Glasgow. Had Seoras really been part of that team? Well maybe the team had been more like that, but Hope was sure Seoras hadn't been. He had changed over the last years, though.

Hope got into the car, sat down, and put a hand to her belly. Perry got in from the other side, and she started for a moment, taking her hand away. Perry had clearly looked, but he didn't say anything as he started the car up, for the short drive back to the spa.

'What?' said Hope. 'You can say it.'

'I think I've said enough tonight,' said Perry. 'I've already upset Jona.'

'Say it!'

'I hope it works for you,' said Perry. 'It's awkward when you don't know.'

Hope simply turned to look away out of the car window. Next time, she was bringing Ross. Ross didn't pick up on these things, didn't understand people that way. Perry was annoyingly good at it.

Chapter 04

Hope stepped out of the car and found McNeil approaching again.

'I'll give you a little brief,' he said, 'before we do anything else. I got the information you asked for from Maddy Lyle.'

'Take it away,' said Hope.

McNeil led her inside the spa and then pointed down a corridor, taking her into an office. It was sparsely laid out. McNeil advised that this was one that could be used by the guests. There was a computer, with internet access, a printer, television and other such facilities. McNeil thought it would be a good place to start as an office for the team.

'I usually like offices that are off the premises, but if this is what we've got, this is what we've got, we can root out accommodations later.'

McNeil closed the door once Perry had entered as well, and Hope sat down on the edge of the desk, leaving McNeil standing. He pulled out a notepad and then gave a slight cough, as if ready to begin his speech.

'Okay,' he said. 'Currently there's only four guests in this . . . resort. That's normal. They don't have that many guest accommodations.'

'How big are the guest accommodations?' asked Hope.

'They've got like little flats,' said McNeil. 'I mean it's very upmarket, and the stuff in them, it's quite something. There's no alcohol though.'

'Well, that's disappointing,' said Hope. 'I think I'd like more than that for the money they're paying.'

McNeil gave a smile. 'So you've got four guests and you've got five staff members that live here. There are other people that come in for cleaning and that. I'm going through them with our own local force to see where they were. However, the others are here more of the time, so they're the ones to be looked at first.'

'Go on then,' said Hope,

'Okay, for the guests, we've got Celeste Beaumont.'

'Celeste Beaumont,' said Perry suddenly,

'Yes, Celeste Beaumont,' said McNeil.

Hope turned and looked at Perry. 'Should I know her?'

'Hollywood A-list actress. I mean she is right up there,' said Perry. 'Probably more known to me because she'd have been in her starring roles when I was, well, a younger man. She's had a high-profile divorce recently.'

'That's correct,' said McNeil, 'however, the reason she's here is apparently she's preparing for a physically demanding role.'

'That's interesting,' said Perry, 'because she used to do stuff like that when she was younger. As she got older, she did less and less of it, but, well, to be frank, that sort of action woman figure made her name back in the day. Although nowadays, I'm not sure she'd really fit that role.'

'So what's she like then?' asked Hope.

'Oh, she's a cracker, some body on her,' said Perry, and then stopped.

'I meant as an actress,' said Hope.

Perry put his head down for a moment, clearly a little embarrassed at his outburst. When he raised it again, he gave Hope a smile.

'She made her name doing action movies, and to be quite frank, they weren't the greatest, nor did they have incredible dialogue. However, they were well liked by certain age groups, a young-male demographic, if you understand me. So, as an actress, well, she's okay, and she can act; she's not rubbish, but she's no Judy Dench.'

'But as a movie star?' asked Hope.

'As a movie star, she's stacked in all the right places, or at least she was,' said Perry. 'Sorry,' he said. 'I know it's not PC to say that, but—'

'But it's very relevant,' said Hope. 'Who else have we got?'

'We've got Jack Harrison, the Hammer. He's a former heavyweight boxing champion.'

'I have heard of him though I don't follow boxing,' said Hope. 'What's he doing here?'

'He's lost the last couple of fights, so he's preparing for a comeback. They've got cutting-edge physical therapy here, apparently.'

'I have no idea what that means,' said Hope. 'You don't hear many boxers going to spas before they—'

'It's a possibility, though,' said Perry. 'Alternative treatments. If he lost his fight, it might not be the physical edge. It might be the mental edge. Just a thought.'

Hope nodded and then give a smile again to McNeil, showing he should continue.

'The next one's an interesting one. Sir Edward Pembroke.

He's an ex, well, a recently retired, Intelligence Officer dealing with stress-related health issues.'

'Stress-related health issues,' said Hope. 'As a spy. I thought they just came with the territory. They all have them, don't they?'

'Specifically, Maddy says that he's got a paranoia about his past catching up with him.'

'Like you say,' said Perry. 'Doesn't that go with the territory for a spy?'

'What age is he?' asked Hope.

'Older. Quite an endearing man in some ways, from what I've seen,' said McNeill. 'Not that I've spoken fully to him.'

'And who else?'

'Well, the last one is Zara El Amin.'

'Zara the what now?' asked Hope.

'Zara El Amin. She's a Middle Eastern princess.'

'Get out,' blurted Hope. 'A Middle Eastern princess on the Isle of Harris.'

'Nobody's meant to know she's here,' said McNeil. 'This is the one that Maddy's most worried about getting out. Apparently their clientele, your A-listers and that, if they're seen being in therapy, ultimately, that doesn't do them any harm press-wise. You've seen that,' said McNeil. 'So Maddy says, you know, yeah, they've done drugs, now they're in getting treatment. It makes great press. This lady, actually more of a girl, Zara is a Middle Eastern princess escaping family pressures and recovering from an addiction.'

'What sort of an addiction?' asked Hope.

'Maddy's very loathe to say. I pressed her and I think it's drug related.'

'Okay.'

'She's said to me several times, "Zara's name can't get out." I think the clientele from the Middle East pay proper money, really good money. She's worried about losing them. Currently, they see this place as a quiet and under-the-radar place to ditch their struggling family black sheep. After all, most people out here wouldn't recognise any of them. But the press could soon make a meal of it.'

'That's understood. Keep the lid on stuff then, Sergeant,' said Hope. 'What about the staff?'

'Maddy Lyle. You met her. Thirty years of age. She's originally from Edinburgh,' said the Sergeant. 'Not that much I've garnered from her. She seems to be the boss around here. Really, the boss. Not just Spa Manager. She's quite forceful, though she's been courteous to me. But she's constantly pushing her own way.'

'Okay,' said Hope. 'Make sure she doesn't get in the way.'

McNeil grinned. 'Beyond that, there's a Skye Anderson. A twenty-five-year-old Welsh lady.'

'What's she like, then?' asked Hope.

'She wears a lab coat. This is quite something,' said McNeil. 'Don't take this the wrong way, especially after what Perry's just said, but she's twenty-five. She's got long, red hair. She's wandering around in the lab coat. Underneath that, she's dressed in what I would say is clothing that shows her figure. But then, that's everybody here.'

McNeil stopped for a moment and put down the pad. 'I hope you don't mind me saying this,' he said. 'If you were going to do the spa as a TV program, especially one of those American ones, well, Perry wouldn't be in it. You would. You'd probably have Miss Nakamura in it. I mean, she's a young, good-looking woman. Macleod wouldn't be in it because he's grumpy.'

'What do you mean that Jona and I would be in it?'

Perry stepped in. 'Think about it. If you're running an American TV program, it's going to show the police force, our investigation team. He's right. I wouldn't be in it. And this is no reflection on ability, because what they would look at is appearance. So you'd be in it, Jona would be in it, Macleod would be out because he's a grumpy git.'

Hope raised our eyebrows at that one.

'Don't repeat that to him,' said Perry. 'Ross would be in it, because he's a very good-looking man. And the fact that he's gay also helps on the TV. You wouldn't get Clarissa. Sabine Ferguson, probably. Emmett, maybe—I haven't met him. Yeah, and Patterson, Patterson would get in. It's all about people who look good. In fact, with your scar, Hope, you'd probably get turned down, come to think of it. What Peter's trying to say is that considering they're meant to be offering world-class treatments, it's amazing that they find people that all look so good at the same time. But maybe that's the thing. You know, we're dealing with the beautiful people here, aren't we?'

'I've no idea who those people are you talked about,' said McNeil, 'but you're coming from the right place.'

'So Skye's a bit of a looker,' said Hope.

'I'm not being funny,' said McNeil. 'But it's ridiculous. And when I say you're a bit of a looker, it's not just people who are good-looking. You're not getting people who are genuinely girl-next-door, or boy-next-door, who look good. You know? It is very specific. Look good in the movie sense.'

'Okay,' said Hope, 'so who else have we got?'

'There's a receptionist,' said McNeil, 'only it's a man, Alasdair Ross. Fairly young, mid-twenties, again. You'd pick him in a modelling contract. There's a pool and sauna attendant, which was how Maddy described him, Ruairidh Morrison, late teens but again physically looks great. And then you have a seaweed treatment specialist,' said McNeil, emphasising the words, 'Saoirse O'Brien. An Irish lady. It's a very young vibe around here, very, well . . .'

'What?' asked Hope.

'I'm trying to think of the word that I'd use to describe it. You know it's a spa, and yes, you look at the building and you think it's clinical. But it's not clinical vibe that comes off—vibe's the word isn't it,' said McNeill, 'that they use these days—vibe, feeling, whatever, it's, it's—'

'Sexy,' said Hope. 'You're trying to say it's sexy. We're in a sexy spa.' She grinned.

'Yes, sexy,' said McNeill. 'And I feel bad saying that because, you know, everything nowadays is not meant to be about it, but here it's, well, it's like the movies. We all say it's not about it, but it is.'

'That sounds good,' said Hope. 'Thank you for that. That sounds really good. I'm going to meet the guests in the group initially, but I'm also going to need accommodation.'

'I'll get the reception manager, Alasdair, on it. I talked to him earlier, asking about it, because he knows the area. I'm up in Stornoway, so I don't know the area as well. Obviously, we're covered down here, but I'm down because of the incident.'

There was a knock on the door.

'Come in,' said Hope.

Maddy Lyle entered the room with hips that were swinging. Hope couldn't have entered the room in a more look-at-me fashion if she tried. She, however, kept the smile back and gave a rather grumpy, 'Can we help you?' to Maddy Lyle.

'I just thought to say that we really should get round to

seeing the guests. It's getting late and we don't want them to be missing their sleep. They're preparing for treatment tomorrow.'

'I'll talk to them when I want to talk to them, Miss Lyle,' said Hope. 'So, they'll stay up and they'll be happy about it.'

Maddy gave a false smile and said, 'of course.' She went to turn away, but Hope stopped her.

'Oswaldo, tell me a wee bit about him.'

'Well, of course. We called him Ozzy,' she said, smiling. 'And he came over when he was requested by a sheik. We brought him in because he was so good and the sheik was so happy. That's why I gave him a contract.'

'What does he do? Or rather, what did he do?' asked Hope.

'Many different treatments. He's a specialist in that sense. Able to reach and to lift people up. Develop mind and soul at the same time.'

Hope realised that the answer said absolutely nothing, but she could explore that topic later.

'He's been so good with the clients. I don't know a lot beyond his background, except that we had to get him a visa to work. That was handled by one of our guests at the moment, Edward Pembroke.'

Hope raised her eyebrows. 'Was Oswaldo working with Pembroke when he's been here?'

'Yes, indeed.'

'Let me see his quarters before we go any further, if you will.'

Maddy asked Hope to follow her, but as they were walking down the corridor with McNeil, they were stopped by a young man.

'Detective Inspector, this is Alasdair Ross, my reception manager,' said Maddy. 'What is it, Alasdair?'

'The sergeant asked me to see about accommodation. I've got some sorted. That's a house that you can rent,' he said.

'Sergeant, sort out the details with Mr Ross, if you would,' said Hope. 'Lead on, please, Miss Lyle.'

Hope spent the next twenty minutes being shown round a couple of rooms that were bland, in the least. Oswaldo's accommodation wasn't particularly exciting, although it was clean and certainly functional. There was a bed, a small kitchenette, but what Hope noticed most was that in the quarters there were no links to his past. There was nothing outside of what Oswaldo would use day-to-day at the spa.

'Didn't have many knick-knacks then, Oswaldo?'

'Didn't bring any with him,' said Maddy. 'Brought a small bag at the time. Built his life up from here.'

'Right,' said Hope. 'Not a lot to discover about him then.' She stood in the room for a moment. 'Can you leave me just a second? I just want to check round the room on my own,' she said.

'Of course,' said Maddy. Hope watched her leave the room. The last time Hope swung her hips like that, she'd been enticing John. And she certainly didn't walk with that much of a swagger.

Perry stood behind Hope, gazing around the room.

'What do you think?' asked Hope.

'Well,' said Perry, 'we've got a dead man that's come from afar. We know nothing about him except to get him here, a Service employee has helped to bring him. There's absolutely nothing here to tell us about his past life. And everything about his present life is related to the job.'

'You think somebody's cleaned the room up?'

'Maybe. But if they haven't, Oswaldo had a spotless life. And

I mean that in the sense of, he made sure nobody knew where he'd been or what he'd done.'

'That's what I'm thinking,' said Hope. 'I think this is going to be much bigger than just a simple killing. Something's going on here and as of yet, I've no idea what. But there's a story behind what's going on, and we need to find it.'

Chapter 05

ope prayed that the sergeant had sorted out the accommodation so she could just roll into bed. It's one of the things that she found about the job. She went from being in a secretive paradise with John to suddenly working like there was no tomorrow. But that was the thing about these cases. You had to get on top of them quickly. Sometimes you lost vital evidence if you weren't there. And sometimes it didn't make a difference. But you could never tell that at the start.

'I'll just get Maddy then,' said Perry, leaving Hope in the corridor on her own. Her hand almost instantly went down to her belly again, clutching just below her midriff. 'Maybe,' she said to herself. 'Maybe.' She must have been standing there for a few moments because when she looked up, Perry was at the other end of the corridor, saying nothing. He seemed to be keeping a respectful distance.

'You ready for me?' she asked.

'Yes,' he said. 'Thought you could do with a moment.'

Hope was all ready to get defensive, but this was Perry. She'd accepted that Perry could see things. He could spot brief moments in people's lives. He came up with theories based

on these observations that were insanely accurate at times—
although he wouldn't always get it completely correct.

'Our secret,' said Hope to him.

'That's not me,' said Perry. 'I don't tell people private stuff. I
don't band about theories unless you need them.'

'Thank you,' said Hope, as she strode up the corridor. Perry
led her through to a comfortable living room, where Maddy
awaited her.

'Welcome to our common suite. This is where everyone
can mix. It's a good place during the day outside their private
accommodation. I thought it was appropriate that no one was
in anybody else's area,' she said. 'They can get very touchy
about that.'

Hope simply nodded and then followed Maddy across the
wonderfully spacious room. There were sofas that certainly
didn't come from that shop which was forever giving dis-
counts.

The money spent in here was incredible, Hope thought.
There were bowls of fruit constantly available, but other
healthy snacks too. Spread around was plenty of reading
material, and daily papers. There was a TV with headsets
so that you wouldn't disturb anyone else if need be. Computer
access. Comfortable sofas and a fire burning in the corner.

'We don't put the fire on unless someone asks for it,' said
Maddy as Hope gazed at it. 'You have to tread a careful line.
Some of them are highly environmental, so you have to burn
the right stuff.'

Hope looked around the room and in the far corner was a
young Middle Eastern woman. Her skin was dark, but not so
dark that it made hope think of Africa. It was definitely more
of a Middle Eastern feeling. That was one thing about coming

from Northern Europe. When you ventured outside of even Europe, you just got lost in the skin colours and tones. A lot seemed to jam together.

Same with the accents. Europeans talked of an American accent, and yet there were so many different ones. Almost as bad as the UK. Hope's own Glaswegian accent had been refined, but it was still there, and it was nothing to be ashamed of, she thought.

The girl, obviously Zara El-Amin, glanced at Hope quickly and then turned her head away. She wore flowing robes, understated, yes, but perfectly tailored. Her long black hair rolled out across her shoulders, and her eyes were deep and sullen. If she'd been on drugs, it certainly hadn't affected her yet, not as far as a quick observation could tell.

There was a man sitting on a sofa, looking rather glum. He had square shoulders, a chin that was neatly defined, and a nose that clearly had been broken. This must be the boxer, thought Hope, but she didn't engage him yet, instead preferring to turn and survey the rest of the cast.

There was an older man with greying hair swept neatly to one side above what Hope thought were rather large ears. He wore a suit, with a waistcoat underneath. Maybe that was because he was meeting her, but there was also a handkerchief in a breast pocket. He smiled across at her, giving her a measured nod. In some ways, he made Hope think of Anna Hunt, the Service woman. Perfectly cordial, and yet when Hope watched her, she swore there was something more behind Anna.

And then in the room's corner, with long, flowing, blonde hair—wearing a dress that Hope thought was more for going out on the town—stood an older woman, probably in her forties, but nonetheless glamorous. She smiled and Hope wondered where all these perfect teeth had come from. Did people actually pay to get more than just their teeth looked after? To get them whitened up?

Hope was never that sort of person. She liked a bit of glamour, by all means. She was quite happy with wearing things that defined her body, showing off the splendid physique that she had. But she felt this was plastic, taken to a far-off level.

'Perry,' she asked, 'Why is that woman dressed like that?'

Perry grinned back at her. 'That's Celeste. I suspect it's because she's meeting us. She never appears without looking fabulous.'

'And does she always have that much cleavage on show?' asked Hope.

'In the films,' said Perry. 'Definitely in the films. I think as a younger man that may have been one of the big attractions.'

Hope looked to see if he was making a joke but Perry was incredibly level. She realised he was being deadly serious.

'Does she still do it for you?' asked Hope.

'No,' said Perry, trying a little too hard, 'I think I've migrated in my tastes.'

'To what?' asked Hope.

'More natural women.'

Hope smiled. Perry would not give too much away, and he was working hard to say that ever so politely,

'If I can have your attention,' said Hope, 'please grab a seat here in front of me. There are plenty of sofas, if you need one for yourself.'

Zara didn't move from a position in the far corner, but the man Hope thought was Jack Harrison sat down directly in front of her. He looked annoyed. Celeste strode over as if there was a row of paparazzi taking photos and then sat, crossing her legs, but making sure that the slit in the skirt had them to mid-thigh. Hope wondered if she realised that this was an informal police interview.

The man who looked like a spy and who Hope reckoned was Edward Pembroke strode over and sat down directly beside Celeste. He paid her no attention, though, and focused directly on Hope. Maddy stood off to one side, ever the perfect host.

'Apologies for keeping you up to this late hour,' said Hope. 'I hope we'll be able to let you go soon. I will, however, need you to remain on site at this time.'

'It's Ozzy though, isn't it?' said Jack. 'Right. Ozzy's bloody dead.'

'We believe that Mr Hernandez is the victim. The Forensic team are working on the scene. I don't wish anyone to leave until I get that forensics report. I'll also be interviewing you but given the hour, we'll do it tomorrow. I would suggest you all go and get a decent night's sleep.'

'There's no point being here,' said Jack.

'And why is that?' asked Hope.

'Because Ozzy's gone. I'm here for treatment, here to get sorted. I'm not here to sit around and enjoy myself.'

'Sir, I'm not here to enjoy myself either,' said Hope. 'I'm here to solve what is a potential murder. So, you'll kindly remain until I have interviewed you tomorrow.'

'Bloody joke,' said Jack. 'Don't see why the—'

Edward Pembroke stood up and calmly walked over the few paces to where Jack was sitting.

'You need to sit, and you need to let the authorities do their work.'

'You don't get off on telling me, Grandad, what to do.'

'Just sit and let the lady inspector continue with her work.'

'Inspector. Why the hell do we get women inspectors?'

Could he be such a dinosaur at such a young age? thought Hope.

'I'm out of here tonight,' said Jack Harrison

'No, you won't be,' retorted Edward. 'You'll sit there like a good lad and you'll do whatever you're asked.'

Jack sprung to his feet in quick fashion and Hope saw one leg go in front of the other in a boxer's stance. The fists now were clenched.

'I'll bury you, old man. You don't tell me what to do, okay?'

'Let's all take a seat for a moment,' said Hope quickly. Harrison's hands were huge. She certainly wouldn't want to get caught with a punch from them. However, Pembroke didn't seem bothered at all, merely adjusting his tie and then sitting down again beside Celeste.

'Well,' said Celeste, 'I don't mind staying, just as long as the press doesn't get in. I'll be happy to remain. As soon as they come, I'm out of here.'

Hope wondered if that was true. After the press came, the centre would be big news.

'One thing I would like to ask,' said Hope. 'Which of you were getting treatment from Mr Hernandez before he died?'

'Well, I was,' said Celeste.

'Me too,' said Jack. 'I just said that.'

'I was,' said Edward.

Hope stared over to Zara. She said nothing, but she did nod. Clearly, the girl was shy, but she wasn't stupid. Given the nature of the others, though, Hope could understand why the girl stayed on her own, in the far corner of the room.

'What sort of treatment were you getting?' asked Perry.

'None of your business, is it?' said Jack. 'Don't need to know that.'

'It seems to me,' said Edward, rather smugly, 'that Mr Harrison is getting treatment for some sort of stress. He's awfully worked up.'

Jack jumped to his feet. He strode over quickly as Edward stood up, his fist drawn behind him. But Perry moved over quickly.

'There's no need for—'

Jack swung a punch. It caught Perry square on the chin, and Hope saw her constable fall backwards, lights out, onto the carpeted floor.

'And this one's for you, old man,' said Jack. He raised his fist again, but before he could react, Edward hit him straight in the throat with two fingers, causing Jack to buckle and gasp. He stepped back and hit the floor on his backside.

Edward reminded Hope of Anna Hunt indeed. She could move quickly. She'd conceal everything about herself until she needed it. Edward clearly had skills.

'Oh, dear God,' said Celeste, standing up for a moment and then beginning to stumble. Maddie swept in, putting an arm around her, holding her upright.

'I'll take her back to her room,' said Maddy.

'Sergeant,' shouted Hope, and from outside the door, Sergeant McNeil stepped in.

'I'm going to need a little help and get a couple of your constables. Constable Perry is momentarily out of service.'

Hope stepped forward, using all six feet of her height, staring at Edward Pembroke and Jack Harrison.

'If the two of you don't want to spend the rest of the night in a cell, I suggest you calm down. Mr Pembroke, I kindly ask that you will not, I say again, not provoke Mr Harrison. I will interview you all tomorrow. In the meantime, to your rooms, and no trouble from any of you.'

Again adjusting his tie, Edward Pembroke turned to Hope and said, 'My apologies, I think my friend got a little out of hand. I shall, of course, be delighted to speak to you tomorrow. Good night.' With that he turned, crisply walked out of the room, while Harrison sat on the floor still choking.

'You keep your fists to yourself,' said Hope. 'And don't go after that man. It won't end well.'

Harrison grunted. 'Get the bloody hell out of here,' he said. She went to help him up, but he pushed her hand away and then stormed off. Meanwhile, Hope turned to see one of the police constables down on his knees helping an incredibly woozy Perry get up to his feet.

'Damn,' he said. 'What the hell was that?'

'That was a world-class boxer laying one on you. Apart from hitting the canvas, I thought you took it well,' said Hope. Perry was feeling his jaw. 'I'm going to get that checked to see if it's broken,' she said.

'I've asked for an ambulance to come out,' said McNeil. And then he took a quick step, steadying Perry, before helping him down to one of the sofas.

'You stay there until they check you,' said Hope. Perry gave no argument, and Hope walked over to the window of the lounge. Everywhere was dark outside, except for the closest areas, the grass lit up by the lights. It wasn't the grass you normally saw here, but perfectly manufactured.

What on earth am I dealing with? thought Hope. *Here, in the wilds, here, in this strange piece of perfection, with four people who don't seem to get on.*

It was then she stopped and noticed that Zara hadn't moved.

'You can go to your room if you wish,' said Hope. The shy young woman simply nodded, trying not to maintain eye contact as she left, her flowing robes making her look elegant, if young.

This is going to be a fine one to explain to Macleod, thought Hope. *I've only just arrived here, and we've already had a fight. Still, he will be coming. Amazing. Maybe he can knock some sense into these people.*

Chapter 06

Hope sat with her feet up on the coffee table in the lounge of the rented house. It was the early hours of the morning, and Perry was crashed out on the sofa, mobile in his hand. His chin was sporting a bruise, and she thought it would get worse. However, the medic said it wasn't broken, but it would really sting for a while.

Well, that was good, because she didn't want Perry having to spend the night up at the hospital. More than that, she couldn't keep him on with a broken jaw. He'd need time off to get treatment, and with Susan Cunningham already getting her prosthetic dealt with, Hope would be too many people down. Macleod, no doubt, would draw on the other teams he had. But God forbid he'd actually send over Clarissa to help.

She got results, she got things done, but Hope struggled with Clarissa. She was rough and ready and often did things that Hope wouldn't approve of. Now that they were each running separate teams, it was a lot smoother than it had been with the two of them working side by side. Yes, Clarissa had been on the same level as her and thankfully not tried to impose a parity of rank between them. Now that she had her own team to run alongside Hope's, the relations between them were much more cordial.

Perry was on the phone. However, he wasn't saying much, because every time he spoke, he seemed to wince. Someone else, however, was speaking away to him.

'Who's that?' mouthed Hope over to him.

Perry went to speak back and then winced. So instead, he held up a hand with two fingers pointing down. He then lifted one of the fingers up halfway. It was Susan. The team member who was missing half a leg. Hope knew she was off to get her prosthetic. Was that today? It was, wasn't it? It actually was today. She'd been away for a little while and it took time to fix these things if that was the right way to be thinking about it. But she'd been fast-tracked by Anna Hunt, according to Macleod. And when Anna did something like that, he made sure that Susan was ready.

Hope held up her thumb, asking if it was going well, to which Perry tried to give a beaming smile, and then winced again. Eventually, he gave up and just put his thumb in the air. *Well, that was something,* thought Hope. *At least somebody's having a good day.* She's picked up her own phone and called Macleod.

'You know what time of day it is?' said Macleod.

'I'm very well aware of what time of day it is. But this day started some time ago,' said Hope, 'and right now I think I've been on the move for, ooh, possibly twenty-four hours.'

'Why did your day start at three in the morning?' asked Macleod.

Hope suddenly stopped. Yes, it had started at three in the morning, but there wasn't any work reason. She gave a brief smile to herself, because the reason had been a good one, and an enjoyable one. But now she was at work, and she needed to focus.

'I take it you're not in bed then yet,' said Hope.

'I'm still in the office, finishing stuff up. What have you got for me?'

'Well, we had an interesting evening. I'm off to see Jona to see how far she's got. She's probably going to be working right through the night before she heads up to Stornoway with the body.'

'Well, give her my best,' said Macleod. 'I'll be over soon.'

'You're going to enjoy this one. We've got four guests here. Celeste Beaumont. Ever heard of her?'

'The actress, yes.'

'Well, Perry's an expert,' said Hope. She glanced over at Perry. He winced as he smiled again. 'She looks like one of these ones who likes the limelight. I'm not too sure how she fits into all this, but never say never. We've got Jack Harrison, a boxer, wo picked a fight tonight with one of the other guests. Perry interceded and took one right in the chin. Cracking punch too.'

'Is he okay?' asked Macleod.

'He's fine. Well, he's got a stonking bruise coming up on his chin. And he's struggling to speak properly, but it's not broken. I'm sure he'll be all right when he gets a bit of rest.'

'When you go to see Jona, leave him. Tell him to get to bed, get some sleep.'

'I'll tell him to throw some painkillers in as well. The guy that Jack Harrison was trying to hit is a Sir Edward Pembroke, former service. When Perry had been floored, Harrison went to punch Pembroke. Pembroke reacted by jabbing him in the throat.'

'In the throat? What age would you say Pembroke was?'

'Sixties?'

'So a neat move,' said Macleod. 'He really is Service then.'

'I think he's ex-Service,' said Hope, 'and I also think that he was active, out and about, not a desk-Service person. But he's not talking about it. He's acting as if he still is part of the Service, telling people to stay calm and follow the authorities. But I'm not convinced. There might be something more behind him.'

'And there's a fourth one, isn't there?' said Macleod.

'Young woman. Zara El-Amin. Incredibly shy. I'll get to talk to her tomorrow, but she's in her late teens. She really is not the most forthcoming—stayed away from the rest of them.'

'I'm going to see someone before I come down' said Macleod. 'I'm still getting plenty of heat here about it, so make sure you keep the press back when they get there. Have you seen any yet?'

'No,' said Hope, 'but it's probably starting to leak now. I'm sure in the next day or so, they'll arrive. It's not that easy getting over here.'

'That's a bonus,' said Macleod, 'but just be aware because it's coming.'

'What about your end? Ross got anything. I have had no contact with him.'

'He was off doing that thing with his kid. Sent me some stuff though. He's been working from home. Says he'll be there tomorrow.'

'What's he saying, though? He hasn't emailed anything through yet.'

'Oh, it's only just come to me,' said Macleod. 'Apparently your spa's big business, and I mean big, big business.'

'You get that feeling here with the people that they're looking after.'

'When they built it,' said Macleod, 'there were local objections to the site, which I can understand. I mean, it's the east side of Harris. The place is amazing to look at. The rocks like the far side of the moon. It's fantastic.'

Hope couldn't get used to people even saying that. She never clocked initially as a moonscape. But then again, she'd never been there. Neither had Macleod been on the moon either.

'Local objections, however, were overruled. And at the high level. The really high level. Top government. Place was constructed quickly, Ross says, with outside contractors.'

'Well, that's fair enough,' said Hope. 'I mean, some of the materials wouldn't be available locally. You wouldn't—'

'No, all outside contractors. Complete lockdown, making sure that there were no leaks out of what went on, what happened. They were making it to look like a . . . not a fortress, but a secret hideaway for clients.'

'Well, that's different,' said Hope. 'So I take it there's been a few objections locally since then.'

'To be honest, I haven't looked at the photographs.'

'It is an eyesore,' said Hope.

'That part of the world is different. You really are right away from stuff. I guess in that sense it's easy to keep your head down and to not be noticed. So location wise it's perfect. There's an airport close by. You could also take clients from there out in a helicopter. The airport's used to dealing with bigger clients if need be.'

'And the food and necessities, are they coming from the island?'

'That was part of the problem. Lots and lots of it shipped in. There's very few locals work there, and they were vetted very, very carefully. I doubt many of them are going to say much, or give much away. They'll get bonuses for keeping stum.'

'As long as they don't keep stum from us.'

'Just be aware of it,' said Macleod.

'So,' said Hope. 'I haven't really gone anywhere. I'm going to start the interviews tomorrow. I'll get off to see Jona now, to find out what she's discovered. I feel like it's the calm before the storm.'

'Sounds like you've had a storm already,' said Macleod. 'Keep me updated.'

'You staying at the office through the night?'

'No, I'm going home. I'm going to get some sleep, and then I've got to see somebody.'

'About the case.'

'Of course, it's about the case,' said Macleod. 'I'm not going to hang you out to dry. I said I'd be down, and I'll be down, but I need to talk to someone.'

Hope looked over at Perry, who was still on the phone to Susan Cunningham, and so decided to make herself a coffee before going out to see Jona. She made her way into the kitchen, which had a few items in it, and somebody had put milk in the fridge. She made herself a coffee, then came back inside and sat down.

The room was silent except for the occasional murmur from Perry, until Hope heard something at the front door. It sounded like the letterbox. Getting up with a slug of her coffee, she then marched to the front door and found an envelope on the floor.

She stopped for a moment, turning and finding her leather jacket and taking out a latex glove. Picking up the envelope, she took it inside and placed it down on the coffee table. For the first time in a while, Perry spoke, telling Susan that he'd ring her tomorrow as something had come up. In saying that, he mumbled his way through it and had to do it again just so she could understand.

'Just dropped through the door,' said Hope.

'What was that?' said Perry almost indistinguishably,

'Don't know yet,' said Hope. Finding herself a second latex glove, she opened up the envelope slowly. Finally, pulling out a piece of paper from inside, she found cut out on a white page, newspaper letters.

'Rodel Church tomorrow at midnight,' said Hope, reading the words.

'Where's Rodel Church?' asked Perry.

'Didn't you clock it,' said Hope, 'when we came down round through Leverburgh. It's out on the edge.'

'Trap,' said Perry, mumbling,

'Don't know,' said Hope. 'I'll have to go to it though, but if I'm going to go out and do that, I want to make sure it's no trap.'

Perry nodded. 'Anyway,' said Hope, taking off the latex gloves, then walking out to pull out a plastic envelope from inside her jacket. She came back and again carefully, using a latex glove, placed the letter and envelope inside the envelope and set it down. Perry was now standing.

'No you don't,' said Hope. 'I'm going to see Jona. You're going to bed. You need to rest. He hit you with such a punch. At least you weren't concussed.'

'I've had worse,' said Perry.

'What? When?' asked Hope. 'You put your face into a car or something.'

Perry laughed and then grabbed his chin. 'Don't do that,' he said, through gritted teeth.

'I won't,' said Hope. She picked up the envelope and then grabbed her jacket before stepping outside. It had been posted through the letterbox. The house they were in had a bit of a distance around it before the next one, but she was close to Leverburgh now, where there were people. Further round the road, houses were sparser, and that was saying something considering where she was at the moment.

There was a breeze, and Hope felt a chill in the air. She zipped up her leather jacket before getting into the car. As she turned the key, she felt something else. Something she couldn't put her mind to. It came from just below her stomach.

Was she getting butterflies? Feeling something? Was this her mind reacting? She didn't have time for this now. Hope needed to go out to see Jona, and she needed to think. She refocused.

Hope started the car again and then drove the short distance in the darkness. And there was that feeling again. Hope prayed it was true. It was her first time looking to conceive, and she didn't understand how she would feel when it happened. If indeed it had happened. But now, she wondered if this was what it felt like. Or was she just imagining it?

Chapter 07

Hope yawned as she pulled the car up at Loch Ghreosabhagh. For a short while, her lights had been just about the only thing showing along the road. And then suddenly, everywhere was lit up. Jona had clearly got some more lights hired from somewhere. And the steady thrum of the generators providing the energy for the lights gave a slightly surreal feel to the area. As Hope stepped out of the car, she felt a light bit of rain beginning to fall.

'I'm glad to see I'm not the only one at work in the wee hours,' said Jona. Hope looked across to the forensic wagon. Jona was standing at the back and gave a wave. 'Come in out of the rain,' she said. 'I've got the coffee on. I'm just taking five.'

Hope marched across, up into the wagon, and found it to be warm inside because of a fan heater.

'What?' said Jona. 'Got to have your creature comforts out here. Take a seat.' A coffee was passed over to Hope before Jona joined her at the small table.

'You making progress?' asked Hope.

'Is that your way of saying, "What have you got for me? I hope you've got something by now,"' said Jona.

Hope laughed.

'Well, despite being one of the more unusual areas to find a dead body—and being difficult to get at while preserving what's going on—I can tell you that Oswaldo was murdered. But it's not a simple matter.'

'Murder rarely is a simple matter,' said Hope.

'Well, maybe,' said Jona, 'but sometimes the bodies are. You stab somebody, they're dead. It's not that complicated. This one, however, is slightly bizarre.'

'Why?' asked Hope.

'I think he was asphyxiated. There are marks around the neck that seem to show that. But possibly, it was unsuccessful. I also think he's been injected with something. I can see various areas where it looks like something's been punch into him. The thing is, they've gone for the right veins. They know what they're looking for.

'The seaweed wrap, however, is bizarre. It has restorative properties, so they could be looking to heal up puncture marks. But it's a bit of a long shot. There's nothing to say anything will work that well clinically. I still have to get him up to the morgue, though. When I'm up there, I'll be able to work it out. We'll be able to lift the body soon and get it on the move. It's awkward working under a tent out among those rocks. I'm trying to keep the tent balanced and prevent that rain from coming in.'

'I'm sure a professional such as yourself will manage it.'

'There'll be no need to soft-soap me. How are things at your end, anyway?' asked Jona.

'Well, I've got plenty of suspects. And at the moment, I don't really know them,' said Hope. 'I'm interviewing them in the morning. So I'd probably best get back and get some sleep soon.'

'Lucky you,' said Jona. 'I'm going to take hotel rooms up near Stornoway because that's where we'll be working out of, mostly. Especially with the morgue up there. However, we'll be down here most of the time. I'll keep a presence. There's a few of us. Not that many. Don't give me too many sites to look at.'

Hope laughed. 'I don't actually get to tell my murderers what to do.'

'Really?' said Jona. 'Feels like it sometimes. Running here, there, and everywhere, picking up the pieces.'

Hope downed the rest of her coffee. 'Thanks for that. Anything unusual?'

'No. Like I said before, probably dumped from the roadside above. Possibly aiming to make the water, but never did. May have been disturbed, and therefore couldn't come down to finish the job off. It's a remote location, but, well, that's your side of the business?'

'How heavy was he?'

'Oswaldo? Not a heavy man, but he's a fully grown man. You'd have to be reasonably strong to carry him. I mean, most women could probably do it at a push. Men, yes. But if you were really slight, it could be very awkward. We didn't find any traces of seaweed up top. Could be in a bin by now.'

'Send one of your guys over and take a look at the bins.'

'You think they're stupid enough to put it in their bin?' asked Jona. 'Why not stick it in a bin somewhere around here? If you've gloves on, it won't matter. Especially if you use the wrap from the spa.'

'Yes, point taken, but do it for me, anyway.'

'Have you ever thought,' asked Jona, 'why places always name themselves the way they do?'

Hope was up on her feet now, about to go out the door, and she stopped. 'What are you on about?'

'Tides of Tranquillity. It's just begging for it, isn't it? It's just begging for something to go wrong. If you called it, "The Spa Resort," and this happened, it doesn't look ironic, does it? The Tides of Tranquillity.'

'Gets to you out here, doesn't it? Working in the middle of the night,' said Hope. She heard Jona stand and take a swing at the back of her ponytail, knocking it to one side.

'You just be thankful that I come out and I do this, okay? Go and get some sleep.'

For a moment, Hope went to turn back to Jona. She wanted to share about what she had felt. She could call John, but she didn't want to get John's hopes up and then dash them. But this was a feeling she had and this is one of her best female friends. No, might just be something daft. Might just be a flutter she was having.

Jona probably knew she was trying for a kid. She'd never said, but well, Jona was perceptive. Hope had trouble working among a load of detectives. They were perceptive.

Hope continued out to the car, clambered in, and put the wipers on before starting the engine. As she drove back along the winding road into Leverburgh to find her digs, she thought about Jona. The two of them were single women and but she might have a child. How would that be different? Would life with John be different?

In some ways, Hope had never thought about it. She was just taking a jump into this world without planning. Hope wasn't reckless. But neither was she someone to plan everything in life. She'd see a moment and take it. Like when they'd been out all night on the beach at Channery Point after the concert.

They hadn't planned to go there. Hope had decided it and John had run with her. She didn't want to lose that. She didn't want to lose that spark.

Macleod wouldn't have done that. But this was Hope. They said she was by the book as a detective. And yes, in general, she was. But she was also impulsive at times. Not like Clarissa. She wouldn't run in and batter people. She wouldn't just tear the place apart. But if she saw an opportunity, she went for it.

That's what she was doing now, wasn't it? This was her. This is what she was doing. Life was presenting the opportunity. It was a time to have kids. She'd moved up the ranks. She was in a good position financially. Relationship-wise, she was stable.

Hope stopped herself. Stable? She was describing her time with John as stable; she wasn't stable. She was besotted. This was her man, and he, well, he was head over heels with her. This was an opportunity, and she was going to take it. They were going to take it.

Before she'd realised, she was back at the digs and out of the car. Hope went through to find Perry, half dozing in a chair in the living room.

'I told you to go to bed,' said Hope, coming in. 'It was an order, Constable.'

'Bed was up there,' said Perry, pointing up to the ceiling as he mumbled. 'I was here and my eyes shut. Don't worry, I got a few bits and pieces. I'll head up in a minute.'

'I'm going to get some myself,' said Hope. 'I just need a few moments to think things through, and then I'll get off to bed. We'll be going back to interviewing in a few hours.'

'I was thinking about Oswaldo,' said Perry, and Hope stopped. If Perry was talking like that, Perry was about to empty his mind of what he'd been thinking. Maybe more than that. The man was deep, despite his rather strange outer attire. His mind at work could be genius.

'What about Oswaldo?' asked Hope.

'Well, we haven't seen all of Oswaldo's life, have we? The thing is,' said Perry, 'you go into that room and it's sterile. We've got all this time before he arrives here that we know nothing about. There are no photographs. There's nothing there to say, "Look, this is who I was before I came here. This is what I've brought to the party." We know it was that sheik that wanted him, so that's a possible line to follow up, if we can get the name. But there's also, oh, a life lived that we don't know about. We need to find that life.'

'Well, I'm not disagreeing with you there. By the way, he was definitely murdered,' said Hope.

'And wrapped in seaweed. How?' asked Perry.

'Asphyxiated, Jona thinks. But she's not sure if that actually killed him. And she thinks he was injected with something later. She's got to get to the morgue first, before she can tell us in detail.'

'Why wrap him up in seaweed, though? It's got . . . it's got to be something to do with who he is.'

'Well, maybe he was wrapping them up in seaweed previously,' suggested Hope.

'He's not the seaweed guy,' said Perry. 'You've got a seaweed treatment specialist, O'Brien. Irish girl. So, you wrap him up in seaweed to what? Point the finger at her? Because if so, that's incredibly amateurish,' said Perry. 'I mean, nobody in their right mind is going to wrap him up in seaweed if they're the seaweed specialist.'

'Seaweed has restorative properties, though, doesn't it? Jona said that there's a possibility it could heal up the wounds made from the injections.'

'So maybe if they got him into the sea, they thought that would be the case. Or maybe they thought that if he was in the sea wrapped in seaweed, people wouldn't think of him as a body until it was way too late. That would be someone with a thoughtful mind, as opposed to vengeance, as opposed to somebody dumb trying to point the finger elsewhere.'

'Jona thinks they were trying to hit the sea,' said Hope, 'dumping the body down the rocks to the water. She says most people could have carried him back up, unless you were a tiny frame.'

'So, it's unlikely to be our Middle Eastern princess,' said Perry, 'at least not on her own.'

'She looks so scared. I don't think it could be her,' said Hope.

'No. But if Oswaldo was messing about with her, Daddy might have sent somebody over. Good way to go about it. Especially if you're trying to throw him into the sea, so he disappears. Neat and tidy. That's the thing,' said Perry. 'It looks like this should have been a neat and tidy job. The fact he's still there means the finger points at other people. If he just disappeared, you and I wouldn't be here. The police force here is not that big. Would anybody be that bothered? He's just a missing Argentinian. Or Swiss national, actually. And that's where I'm coming from. There's this entire story about where he was born, where he then went to, to become a Swiss national.'

'The other thing is,' said Hope, 'this is not like some of the other cases, is it? You walk in that room, it's like living with the beautiful people.'

'The what?' said Perry.

'The beautiful people. When you were at school, did you not

have the beautiful people?'

'What are you on about?' said Perry.

'When I was at school, there was always this group at the top. And they were always the best looking. They were the coolest.'

'Not being funny,' said Perry, 'but were you not part of that group? I mean, don't take this the wrong way. You got the looks.'

'I was tall and lanky, and had red hair racing down my back that was incredibly long. When I was a teen, I wasn't like I am now,' said Hope. 'You know I don't see myself that way.'

'No, you don't,' said Perry, 'and that does you credit. And I don't mean to say that's who you are.'

Hope could see Perry was struggling here. Ever since he'd come into the team and sounded quite sexist, he was working hard to pull back from any comment, even though he was being quite reasonable in what he was saying.

'The beautiful people—they were the ones that did the coolest things, got to the top, not the geeks, not the nerds,' said Hope. 'This is like the beautiful people now. The thing was, the beautiful people always gave off that front image of being in charge, in control, and being delighted with life, and being fabulous. That's what I think we've got here. I don't think they're in control at all. Why on earth would you be here if you weren't in control?'

'Somebody's in control,' said Perry. 'You don't wrap a body up like that, think about healing people, the wounds, and then chuck them in the sea, to give that air of disappearance, as opposed to murder, if you're not in control. This was not a rash act. This was done by somebody who thinks well, who plans to a degree. Maybe they had to do it quickly, but there's an element of planning.'

Hope looked at Perry for a moment. 'You know what that means, don't you?'

'It means as the story develops, as we get closer, this person could react in a planned way too, throw us off the scent, not just lash out wildly; makes them harder to find, harder to spot.'

'You'd better get to bed Perry; me, too. Let's see if we can find our killer in the morning.'

Chapter 08

'At least, put your coat on.'

Macleod shook his head and strode out of the rear of his house onto the patio to sit down in an outdoor chair. It was dark, very dark, but the lights from the house lit up the patio to a degree. There were still shadows out there, everywhere, and with no moon shining tonight, he was struggling to see the Moray Firth through the trees.

He liked that about the house. You could see the water through the trees on a good day, and yet there was plenty of shade if it was too sunny. Macleod didn't like the sun, but he certainly didn't like this November darkness. He had his dressing gown wrapped around him tightly, slippers on, and hadn't really slept for the last three hours after he'd got the text message.

It was a text message at one in the morning, which meant he'd almost leapt out of bed thinking something was up. As he'd read it, he'd felt the arm come across, pulling him closer. A voice telling him she hoped he wasn't running off. That was the thing about Jane; she didn't just look after herself. It would have been very easy to just turn over and go back to sleep.

She had sat with him, or rather lain with him in the bed,

knowing he was awake. Holding him tight when he had said that someone would be coming but she wasn't to worry. He'd hoped he'd given her enough information.

Jane had a very unusual relationship with those who Macleod worked with. She knew Hope well, for Hope had saved her life once. But the others were more at a distance, and Macleod was glad of that. This team saw things that Jane didn't need to see, and although she'd had her moments living with him—which had brought her into some situations she shouldn't have been in—he liked that distance.

He didn't share all the horrors he saw. He talked more about the people, the fascination of character, and she would listen, and sometimes offer her own thoughts. But she let him be the inspector. But when he was home, he was her Seoras. She was his respite from it all.

A respite he hadn't had for so long when he was working down in Glasgow. And he realised it had twisted him. Not wholly, but to a degree. The last lot of years had seen that change. He was a happier man now. More contented. Even happy to be out of the fray to a degree. Who was he kidding? He wasn't happy to be out of it. He just knew how to manage it now.

'I take it they drink coffee as well,' said Jane. She placed in front of Macleod a cafetiere of black coffee and two mugs. 'Is this going to be long?'

'I don't know,' said Macleod. 'They'll be gone before sunup, though.'

'That's about three hours,' said Jane.

'Go back to sleep,' said Macleod. 'Don't wait up. I'm perfectly safe. It's someone I trust completely.'

Jane nodded, and Macleod believed she knew who he was

meaning. Of course, Anna Hunt had been someone Jane had met. It was an easy assumption that when things happened out of the norm, it was Anna that Macleod was speaking to. But Jane also knew that Macleod didn't have complete trust in Anna. He had told Jane she always had her own agenda, and you had to be careful. She was a good woman, but the Service made you go in directions sometimes that weren't wholly compatible with your own inner convictions.

Jane knew that this wouldn't be Anna as she slid down onto Macleod's lap, put her arms around him, and kissed him.

'Put a coat on. It's freezing.'

'You haven't got one on,' said Macleod.

'I'm going back to bed. I'm going to stay warm so that when you get back into bed, there'll be a warm bed to come into,' she said. 'But if you come in like an ice bucket, I will kick you out into that shower.'

Macleod laughed. 'If I have to shower to be allowed into that bed, I shall do it. But I don't need a coat. I'm not that old yet.'

Jane kissed him again, got up, and disappeared into the house. Macleod knew it was all bravado, the talk of the coat. And so did Jane as she returned, inside of a minute, with Macleod's coat. She told him she wasn't leaving until he put it on. Having zippered it up, he sat back down in his chair and poured a coffee. He heard Jane disappear and sat back to await his guest.

'Anna wouldn't like this.'

The voice was beside his ear—his right ear—and Macleod nearly jumped off the chair. How did she do that?

He stood up and turned to see a woman dressed casually in black. Black bomber jacket, black jeans, a black baseball cap even at this time of night, and black boots. He opened his arms and Kirsten Stewart hugged him hard. When they released, she took up the chair beside him and poured herself a coffee.

'It's four in the morning,' said Macleod. 'You're really telling me that you need to move about at four in the morning?'

'You asked to see me. You said you had something that you needed to talk about. That's fine, but you have good links to Anna. Anna wouldn't like this. I'm not in the Service anymore. I don't have to report to her what I've told you. They consider me a threat. Not a nasty threat. I'm not the lunatic out there that I have to stop. But I'm ex-Service,' said Kirsten. 'I know a lot about them. Therefore, I am still a threat. Even though, at times, I can be an ally.'

Macleod shook his head. 'I wouldn't have got on in that world,' he said.

'No, you wouldn't. I think we worked that out last time. Still, it's nice to be back in Scotland, good to be back on the old stomping ground.'

'What have you been doing then?' asked Macleod. Kirsten raised her eyebrows. Her face was lit barely by the light coming out from the house behind them.

'I went to see the grave,' she said, referring to her brother's last resting place. 'You keep it nice for me, thank you.'

'It's not right, you don't get to see it. Don't forget to watch out going though.'

'They'll know it's somewhere I'll come to. But until now, they haven't known I'm here in Scotland, so they wouldn't have watched it. They might, if they find out you've been talking to me. What do you need of me?'

Macleod related the brief details of what he knew about the murder on the Isle of Harris. At the name Sir Edward Pembroke, Macleod could see Kirsten visibly stiffen.

'So that's it. You need to know about somebody from the Service. Why not ask Anna? You've got good links there.'

'Anna is Service,' said Macleod. 'One thing I know about the Service is they don't talk about themselves easily. She will protect the Service if I ask her questions regarding it. I may not get the full information from her.'

'You might not get the full information from me,' said Kirsten. 'I can't compromise myself either.'

'No,' said Macleod. 'But you'll tell me if that's the problem. You'll tell me you can't say something because it leaves you exposed. And I'll accept that. I'll get the truth from you, even though I may not get all the information.'

'One of the things I've always admired about you,' said Kirsten, 'is your assessment of the situation. And you're right, I will give you the truth. But not necessarily all the information. And Anna won't tell you everything I'm going to tell you. In fact, she'll tell you a lot less than what I'm about to tell you. Be careful how you use it. If you use it in a certain way, and she knows it comes from me, you will lose trust with her. She'll be much more wary of you. You'll become a threat. Even though it's a threat from the good side.'

Macleod shook his head. 'If she'd just tell me stuff in the first place, it wouldn't be a problem.'

'No,' said Kirsten. 'From your point of view, it wouldn't be. When you work in the Service you realise it really would be, but here's your information for what it's worth. Everett Pembroke retired from the Service over three years ago,' said Kirsten. 'He's paranoid.'

'Paranoid?' said Macleod. 'How do you mean, paranoid?'

'Paranoid. Therefore, I don't trust your intentions, always, because they may not fit what needs to be done.'

Macleod sipped on his coffee. He was trying not to judge what she was now, but he preferred Kirsten as that hard-working detective. Her life was too much. Perhaps it was more complicated now, and he wasn't sure how to cope with that.

'He's been watched for a long time, but they don't believe he's a risk. He's a genuine paranoid. However, he has secrets of the Service, and he's in a pretty privileged position. The Service let him go. They didn't squeeze him into a job somewhere and say you can be attached to us for the rest of your life. They let him go, free to pursue his own interests.'

'The service released him,' said Macleod. 'I didn't think—'

'"Released" is a subjective term. It doesn't mean released from a contract, everything unbinding. It means don't rock the boat, don't do anything, and if we see you in trouble or you're getting yourself highlighted, or you're getting visits from the wrong people, we'll come along and have a proper chat with you. That's what being released is. However, they don't see him as a risk. I'm released from the Service' said Kirsten suddenly. 'They keep tabs on me, or try to, though I'm not a genuine threat. I'm a friendly threat, if you see what I mean.'

'Imagine you're harder to keep tabs on than others.'

'Of course I am,' said Kirsten. 'I'm a field operative.'

'Was Pembroke a field operative?'

'Very early on, he did some field work, so he's trained.'

'Well, Hope said that he struck out at the boxer down there. Very quickly, the way you do, the way you take people out. Not just a punch, but he went straight into the throat, quickly.'

'Pretty basic stuff, and that sounds like something he could do. But he was actually a specialist in clinical advantage.'

Macleod put his hands up to the air. 'I have absolutely no idea what that means. I take it, it's not about being a medical opportunist.'

'No, he was looking for decisive methods of gaining advantages for operatives, but I don't have access to what. I never did; he would work and report to the higher echelons. I would only see the fruits of what he was talking about if it came down to us and was being rolled out in the training that they gave, or in equipment.'

'Can you find out what he was involved in?' asked Macleod.

Kirsten thought for a moment, and took a long drink of her coffee, before putting the cup down again. She reached over and filled it up again.

'Trouble is, Seoras, the correct answer is yes, I could. I could find out. But if I did that, I would piss off Anna to an immense degree.'

'Why?' asked Macleod.

'Think about it. You have a line into Anna. She's told you to come to her. That way, she can give you useful information. Not everything, because some things she's got to hold back. If you come to me. I'm now acting as a rogue. I am acting for an agency outside of the Service to get information out of the Service. It's not merely what I know. You are happy that I'm talking to you about Edward Pemberton, but what have I told you? Probably most of what she would tell you. She might phrase it a lot differently. She might even warn you off.'

'Warn me off,' said Macleod. 'Why warn me off? What's she got to hide?'

'You might want to arrest one of us for committing a murder? After being let out and released from the Service? Wouldn't go down well. If you went to her, she would make sure that you didn't scrutinise him because she's quite happy with him. He won't be doing this unless he has a very, very good reason. In which case, she doesn't want you finding those reasons out.'

Macleod wrapped his arms around him. It was cold. But not as cold as the detail he was finding out about his relationship with Anna. Of course, he knew it. But, well . . ., when it was put in stark contrast by Kirsten, it said something more. It hit him.

'You don't want me to get that information about him. I'll end up getting visits I don't want. That could escalate into violence that I don't want. I'm on good terms with the Service. Yes, they want to know what I'm doing. And they want to keep an eye on me. But, frankly, they're quite happy to let me go, as long as I don't rock the boat anywhere. As long as I don't surface causing trouble. She'll be annoyed at what I've just done with you, so make sure she doesn't find out. But if she does, well, it'll just confirm to her that my loyalty lies with you, not with the Service. But I know my limits.'

'Do you think he's capable of murder?' asked Macleod.

'He's from the service. Of course, he's capable of murder,' said Kirsten. 'I'm capable of murder. But I choose when to do it. He's paranoid. Like everybody else, you're going to have to ask why he would be doing it. He's probably there genuinely for help if he's paranoid.

These places sometimes they give help to my kind but undercover. It says it's a spa but the others working with him could actually be giving much more, sophisticated treatment. Sometimes, there are things you don't want to be seen in public. By that, I mean even in a confidential public health service.'

Kirsten drained her coffee. 'I'd love to stay,' she said, 'but at the moment I need to be a ghost until I work out what I'm doing in Scotland.' She stood up from her chair and came over and gave him a hug. 'Great to see you,' she said. 'Any time, you know that.'

Macleod gave a nod of his head and pondered for a moment. When he turned round to wave goodbye to her, she was gone.

Chapter 09

Ross would come that day, which would be a boon, because with only Perry and her, covering off all the suspects was proving difficult. Hope had decided to talk to Saoirse O'Brien, the seaweed treatment specialist. She wondered if the woman would be panicked about the fact that Oswaldo was found in seaweed, and would she feel fingers were being pointed at her? As Hope walked in through the entrance, she saw Alasdair Ross behind the reception.

'I'm looking for Saoirse O'Brien.'

'She'll be down in her rooms. I'll take you there,' said Alasdair. He led Hope down several corridors and into what looked like a highly clinical room. There was a treatment table, a shower, other wipe-down tables that could be used for whatever was necessary. There were also a lot of built-in cupboards, but everything was stored away, neat as if the room had a neatness disorder.

'Would you be here, Miss O'Brien?' Alasdair said in a loud voice. From the rear room, a voice came back. 'With you in a minute.'

'I have the detective inspector here. She wishes to speak to you.'

'I'll be right out.'

Alasdair almost gave a bye as he left the room, and Hope stood waiting for Saoirse O'Brien. When she came through, Hope was slightly taken aback. The woman had red hair, tending more towards Ginger, and it rolled down her back in waves. She was smaller than Hope, but she was buxom and curvy. And although she wore a white lab coat, it was open and Hope could see the tight-fitting clothing underneath. She was one of the beautiful people from her school. Hope couldn't shake this feeling. For being on the Isle of Harris, the spa felt like Hollywood.

'Good morning, Miss O'Brien. I'm Detective Inspector Hope McGrath.'

'Saoirse O'Brien,' said the woman, stepping forward. She offered Hope her hand, and Hope shook it. 'Terrible what happened to Oswaldo. He was, well, he was quite charismatic, I guess.'

'You're not, or you weren't a fan of his?'

'We worked in different parts of the spa. He was more into other treatments. I'm not sure exactly all he did. I do seaweed therapy.'

'Regarding that, are you missing some?' asked Hope.

'I'm missing a large amount,' said Saoirse.

'Do you keep records?' asked Hope.

'No, not particularly. It's not that expensive. Not compared to a lot of the other things that I do.'

'What about access to it?'

'Through here,' said Saoirse. She turned on her heel, and Hope noticed she had boots on. Not practical boots like Hope's, but high heels. They must have killed her feet walking about on those. Hope followed her through into another room, where some large crates held seaweed, kept under water.

'And this is your store in here,' said Hope, looking around. 'Seems to be a fair amount of seaweed.'

'You'll notice a couple of the crates are empty at the top, Inspector. I had a delivery only the other day. That's enough to cover a person,' said Saoirse. 'Well, it's actually more than enough to cover a person. I would not be using that amount.'

'Can you give me an amount? A weight.'

'A weight,' said Saoirse, 'for what?'

'For covering a human. The amount you would expect to have used.'

'Of course.' Saoirse turned, went over to a book, flicked it open, and then wrote a number, handing it to Hope.

'Thank you,' said Hope. She would pass it on to Jona and see if they tallied up. 'Are there any precautions in here? Any locks on the doors?'

'No,' said Saoirse. 'It's seaweed. We have locks on the outside. Nobody in here wants to come and take the seaweed. You don't come and do it yourself when you've got a specialist here. Even the staff, if they wanted to do it. Well, we're allowed to give each other treatments to a large degree. It's good. Practise and good experience to understand what's happening,' said Saoirse.

Hope was trying to place her accent. It was possibly the west coast of Ireland. Although, at times, it felt a little forced.

'Are you from Ireland?' asked Hope.

'I am,' said Saoirse. 'My mam's into all this seaweed stuff as well. That's how I got into it.'

'Did Oswaldo ever use the seaweed wraps?'

'Never,' said Saoirse. 'Ozzy didn't do that. That's my job. To be honest, it's not seen as glamorous as what Ozzy was doing.'

'And what was Ozzy doing?'

'Modern, holistic treatment. To be honest, I'm not a hundred per cent sure. I never took any treatment from him, and I was never in with his clients. He didn't like that. Liked none of us about. He worked with them on his own.'

'Do people ever see you do the seaweed wrap here?'

'Oh, often. I'll have other clients come in to watch certain clients, if they're all amenable. I've had staff in. It doesn't bother me.'

'How much of a specialist are you?' asked Hope. 'I don't mean to be rude, but are there any number of people who could do this job?'

'Well, there are others in the world. Of course there are. Plenty. It's a seaweed wrap. You administer it. The magic is in the seaweed, not particularly in my hands. You have to be personable. You have to be—'

Good looking, thought Hope. *How do I put this to her?*

'When you got the job,' asked Hope, 'do you remember any of the other interviewees? Were they around with you?'

'I do.'

'What were they like?'

'Well, they seemed quite nice.'

'What age were they?' asked Hope. 'Would you have said any of them were over thirty?'

'No, we were all fairly young. I think.'

'Men, women?'

'There were a few men and a few women.'

'And qualifications?'

'We submitted those on paper, so I never really found out. There was an interview we got asked back to. There was a board member who came.'

'Don't take this the wrong way,' said Hope. 'Do you think you got your job because of your looks?'

Saoirse blushed for a moment, but then she seemed almost seemed resigned to the possibility. 'Yes,' she said. 'Very much so.'

'That's quite candid,' said Hope. 'Quite a rude question I've asked.'

'I didn't originally go into this type of work. I was doing seaweed wraps back in Ireland for here, there, and everywhere. Loads of different people; a lot of my clientele were people who, well, weren't glamorous at all, but who go for the health option. I saw this job, and I saw the money. I put in for it and I got it, but I did get advised that I needed to look the part.'

'Look the part,' said Hope. 'Who advised you of that?'

'Maddy. She sort of said it to me. Look at me. It's not a female thing. I know the men have been told to dress appropriately, as Maddy puts it. We're meant to be an example of youth and vigour and, well . . . , sexuality.'

'Really?' said Hope. 'That open?'

'Nothing's ever written. But Maddie is here to make sure that the centre looks the part.'

'I don't mean to be rude,' said Hope, 'but does it do the part? Do these treatments work?'

'I can't speak for any of the rest,' said Saoirse, suddenly quite taken aback. 'But seaweed wrap works. This is what I do. This is my livelihood. I would do this if I were back in Ireland with people who were nobody, as opposed to supposed stars who come here.'

Hope was finding the woman quite forward, even to the point where she realised she was being used as an object, as well as a worker.

'How much better is the money?' asked Hope.

'Three times. I have to live away from home, though. We are here at the centre's beck and call. We don't get that many holidays.'

'Turn it back to Oswaldo,' said Hope. 'How was he? Was he liked?'

'Oswaldo was a charmer. It's partly why Maddy liked him here. I think that's why he got the job—as well as his skills, whatever they were. Maddy and Skye were both close to him. They fawned over him.'

'What about yourself?'

'He tried a few times—a few clients have. The clients are a little more subtle about it, but they get told straight. I don't mind being an image but I'm here for the money. I'm here to do several years, build the money up and then do what I want to do. Hopefully set up my practice one day properly.'

'Did he overstep the mark?'

'Are you asking if I killed him? I wouldn't wrap him up in seaweed and dump him off the side of a road if I did.'

'Can seaweed heal marks made by a needle?' asked Hope.

'Take time but it will also help the skin. That's the whole point. Helps the skin to heal up.'

Hope stopped for a moment, thinking about what to ask next, but Saoirse stepped closer to her.

'Look, between you and me, you know what it's like. You've got red hair, and you look good. They want you there. But Oswaldo, Oswaldo was a user. Oswaldo was out for himself. And that's fine. But he would not get me. He got told flat, and he backed off. And we never said any more about it. In truth, I didn't see him that often. I worked very separate from him. I have my rooms here and I have my place to keep separate from him. We don't live in a commune together. I have my flat. It's fine. It's sterile. It's nice. And it does me. I'm doing my time to get what I want.'

'Where were you the evening he died?' asked Hope.

'I was actually out that evening. You can check. Local badminton club down in Leverburgh. It's in the hall. Nothing big or exciting. But I don't exist for this place. I exist for me and what I need to get. And frankly, getting out once or twice a week and mixing with ordinary people is worth it. Alasdair put me in touch with the badminton club. Keeps you fit and you get to see people. You get to talk. Every once in a while, I get to see real people.'

'I won't keep you any longer,' said Hope. 'You're not planning on disappearing anytime soon, are you?'

'It's four weeks before my next break off the island. I think we've got a week when there aren't many clients here, or next to none. That happens, and we all go on our break together. Easier that way. But you don't get to choose your holidays; they give you them. Like I say, it's the money that's brought me here.'

Hope thanked her and stepped back out of the seaweed facility. As she stood in the corridor pondering, she wondered if she could do that. And thought she couldn't. Hope would never be some sort of glamour model, there to be looked at and adored, knowingly. Saoirse had a side to her that clearly was prepared to put up with that. It also said a lot about the place. Back at school, the beautiful people had been false. This seemed to be a false place, too. At least as far as Hope could see.

Her phone vibrated in her pocket. She picked it up, having a look. It was a message from Ross. He'd be with her in twenty minutes.

Chapter 10

ope watched as the police car pulled up with Alan Ross inside. The sergeant stepped out and walked over to his inspector, giving a smile.

'You all good?' asked Hope.

'Yeah, we just had another consultation about the wee man yesterday. Thanks for letting me do that.'

'Not a problem, Alan. You were off anyway. It's Perry and I on cover.'

'Yes, but something like this.'

'Something like this, nothing. Susan would have covered it; except she's off getting fixed up. Anyway, the big boss is over soon.'

Ross nodded. 'What do you need on the case before we go in?' asked Hope.

'Should be okay. Been getting up to speed,' said Ross. 'Been trying to do a lot of the background work as well.'

Hope knew that Ross would have done the background work. He was superb at rounding up all the detail that was available in the public domain about anyone. And in truth, she'd miss that if he hadn't been here.

'Shall we go?' said Ross.

'You don't want five minutes or anything. Sit down with a cuppa. You've been on the go since quite early, I think.'

'Hope, I'm here now. Let's get done,' said Ross.

Hope nodded and went back into the reception to find Alasdair. She asked for Celeste Beaumont, and he took Hope and Ross through to some private quarters. As he opened the door, Hope almost gasped at the living room in front of her. It had everything in it, even a small gym facility at the back.

'Miss Beaumont?' asked Alasdair, into the accommodation.

'I've just finished my shower. I'll be out in a moment.'

'The inspector and her sergeant are here to question you, if that's okay.'

'Of course it is. Get them something to drink. I'll be out directly.'

Hope shook her head when offered a drink, but Ross took a coffee as they sat down in the room. Looking around, there was clearly nothing that was Celeste's. Yet everything was available. There were pictures on the wall that Hope recognised as parts of the outer Hebrides. There was a view out to sea, which Hope then walked over to, standing at the window.

Alasdair poured and gave a cup of coffee to Ross and then joined Hope at the window. 'It's one way,' he said. 'We don't want people looking in on our clients but the health benefits of being able to look out on this every day, even in this weather, well, unmeasurable.'

The view is quite stunning, Hope thought. *Like a little protective bubble though. It doesn't blend in with the island; it is separate from it.*

A door opened, and Hope turned to see Celeste Beaumont enter. The previous evening, she'd been wearing an evening dress, but now she was in a large dressing gown. Even so, the split at the front allowed her legs to walk free and easy. She didn't come over to Hope but sat down on one sofa, crossing her legs, leaving the bottom half of her thigh bare.

'This is Detective Sergeant Alan Ross,' said Hope. 'You remember me from last night. That'll be all. Thank you, Mr Ross.' Hope stopped for a minute. One of the joys about Ross's name was, it was common. Alasdair Ross looked for a moment, realised it was him, and then left the room. Hope sat down beside her sergeant.

'Thank you for seeing us this morning,' said Hope. 'Can I ask why you're here?'

'Here? Like all the rest of us, some rest and some relaxation, just to try to build myself up again.'

'According to rumours,' said Ross, 'that I find on the internet and everywhere else—and I don't take them as gospel—it says that you're here trying to get into action roles. It must be tough at your age.'

Hope thought the comment was quite rude, but maybe Alan had the right idea. Celeste Beaumont, however, didn't bat an eyelid.

'I just need to get a little relaxation. Have you seen any of my earlier work?' she said.

'I'm not that familiar with it,' said Ross. 'I watched about half an hour of one that I caught on the plane on the way over. The flight's not that long, so I couldn't see any more. I have it downloaded; maybe I'll finish watching it tonight,' he said.

'And was I fabulous in it?' asked Celeste.

'To be honest,' said Ross, causing Hope to get slightly nervous, 'it seemed to be more about image than actual story.'

'Of course, it's about image more than story. But when you

have assets such as mine,' said Celeste, almost gazing over her body, 'you're giving the public what they want.'

'The younger male public?' said Ross.

'Well, exactly. We're all in films for a reason. You have to look the part; you have to be fabulous. A bit of rest and I'll look fabulous again.'

'You are getting beyond the age that you were before though,' said Ross. 'Can't be too easy to jump around in your action roles.'

'The stunt doubles are there for the really serious bit. You've just got to present and look the part,' said Celeste.

'What do you mean by that?' asked Hope.

'Oh really dear, come on, a bit of cleavage, a little leg, and a big smile, and make sure that hair is blowing in the wind.'

'How did you find Oswaldo?' asked Hope.

'Well, to be quite honest, I didn't think his treatments were all they were cracked up to be.'

'In what way?' asked Ross.

'He does different treatments, lays his hands on. Some at times I thought were quite intimate, but some of the best ones are.'

Hope found she was being very evasive. 'Where were you the night Oswaldo died?'

'I was in my room—in here early. I was tired.'

'Tired from what?' asked Ross.

'It's a general tiredness. Here to rest and relax. But sometimes, it's not easy. Some of the other guests are a little lively. I think we saw that last night, didn't we, with Mr Harrison?'

'Do you mingle much with them?' asked Hope.

'Well, everybody gets to see everyone on the way round. We

get our meals made for us. The food and everything else is good. It's more than adequate.'

'What did Oswaldo think of you?' asked Hope.

'Oswaldo was a professional. He's doing the treatment. He kept his hands to himself,' said Celeste. Hope wasn't quite sure what she meant by that. Was that a good or a bad thing?

'I found him to be quite, well, he was interested in some of the other women, especially, well, one doesn't like to say, but our Middle Eastern princess, Zara. I think she's a party girl.'

'What do you mean, a party girl?' asked Ross.

'You know the type. I mean, we all go to the parties; we all go to the do's, don't we? Absolutely. But some of us at them indulge a bit too much. I don't mind a bit of the alcohol, but . . .' She pushed her finger up to her nose and sniffed hard at it. 'That sort of thing's not for me. You don't get a body like this by doing that. Got to keep my body the way it is. After all, it's the star of my career.'

'And you say Oswaldo was interested in her?' asked Hope.

'I don't think he was interested in her for her body, although he's a man, so maybe he would have done it on the side. I mean, would you be interested in her?'

Ross was slightly taken aback by the question being so direct, but Hope was proud of him as he rallied.

'I haven't seen her yet.'

'Well, it's one of the dangers of places like this, isn't it? I mean, we all look our best. Sometimes that causes problems.'

Hope wondered where the head was at with some of these people? She was used to real life, where yes, people had affairs, people were attracted, but this was almost laid out like a film. It was almost souped up over the top.

Did Celeste actually believe that most of the men here were desperate to be with her? Well, she'd get an enormous shock with Ross. Is she annoyed that Oswaldo isn't, or hadn't, or had he, and is she now covering up? These people are so plastic, Hope thought, *it is almost difficult to see whether they are faking it.*

Saoirse, she'd got. The woman had seen what the place was, and she was doing a job, earning her living. Money to get out. But Celeste was in this life. This was her.

'Have the press arrived yet?' asked Celeste.

'No,' said Hope. 'We haven't seen any.'

'Good,' said Celeste, almost too forcefully. 'I really can't abide them.'

Hope thought that was debatable. 'Did you ever have the seaweed wrap?'

'Yes,' said Celeste. 'I did. She's quite competent in what she does. I don't think people go for gingers though, do they? They can be a fiery sort of people.'

Now that was rude, thought Hope, *considering a ginger is sitting right in front of you.*

'Getting back to your roles,' said Ross, suddenly. 'Have you been told that you need to smarten up for them? Is coming here part of that? Is it a directive from the film studio?'

'I don't see how that's anything to do with you,' said Celeste. 'I told you I am here for—'

'And you've no addictions or substance issues?' said Ross, interrupting. 'It's just that many people coming here have those sorts of things.'

'I do not. I'm just having a bit of relaxation before I'm back out there. You can't look fabulous all the time. Sometimes you need to be out of the limelight. Even if it's just for a moment. When you spend your life in front of the camera like I do—and it'll be hard for you to understand this—you just need to chill sometimes.'

Hope looked around the room and saw the gym equipment again. There was also gym clothing sitting on Celeste's bed, the door to which was standing open.

'Is there anyone here you didn't get on with? Or you thought Oswaldo didn't get on with?'

'Oswaldo got on with everyone. Oswaldo had that style. And he was always, always, all over the ladies, but he was gorgeous with it, you know. South Americans, though, they have that swagger, don't they, I guess? I think that's what was fantastic about him, that swagger and his attention to detail.

'Like I say, he was very hands-on with the treatments. But sometimes that tension heals you, it's what helps. When you don't have a husband, sometimes you need a therapist who's a little more intimate. Obviously without being—'

'Obviously,' said Ross. He stood up and then looked down at Hope, realising he'd overstepped the mark, but she got her up on her feet quickly, too.

'Thank you, Miss Beaumont. All the best with your future business. We may need to come and talk to you again, just to clarify a few points.'

'Well, I think I've obviously given you all that you need,' she said. 'I wish to get away soon. Obviously, before the press arrives.'

'Obviously,' said Hope, feeling the word was obviously being overused. 'We'll accommodate you as best we can.'

With that, she turned and left the room, followed by Ross. Outside in the corridor, she stopped as he caught up with her.

'What do you think?' asked Hope.

'She's been put here by the studio and she wants the press. She wants attention. But to kill somebody to get the press here would be extreme. She's probably strong enough to move him. She clearly was in intimate sessions with him. Or maybe she wasn't.'

'That a good or bad thing?' asked Hope.

'It's a good story to leak to the press. Sex scandal.'

'One thing I'm finding here, Alan, is everything feels like plastic. It feels fake. The most genuine person I've spoken to here has been Saoirse because she told me it was fake. She told me she was being used as a glamour therapist. Someone who had to play the part. But she knew that because she was taking the money to get out later and get her own larger business set up.'

'Celeste is part of the whole lie, isn't she?'

'Yes, I'm struggling with what this place is, to tell you the truth, Alan.'

'We need to talk to Zara though. Celeste indicated that Ozzy might have been a dealer. I think we need to look at that.'

'It's not uncommon,' said Hope. 'She was talking about the parties, drugs, booze. This may be a health suite but look at it, it's clearly here for them, clearly here for what they want.'

'I wouldn't put it past people to provide them drugs here on the quiet. This place is here to make money.'

'You're right Alan, it's here to make them money. It's not here for their health. Maybe we have to see where the money comes from and goes, maybe see who's making money.' Hope gave a yawn.

'Not much sleep?' asked Ross.

'Start of an investigation? Of course not,' she said. 'Come on, let's go find Alasdair. See if we can find our Middle Eastern princess.'

Ross walked off in front of Hope and Hope found herself

thinking once again about what might be going on inside her own body. It wasn't distracting; it was just every now and again she would wonder.

Chapter 11

Perry was at one of the nearby small harbours, talking to some of the local fishermen. As he wandered down, they stared at him from their boats, wondering who this strange man was. Perry dandered with his hands in his pockets, fidgeting. He had given up the cigarettes, but he still felt the urge. He also struggled now with eating, because he had given up the cigarettes. Out here, he was having difficulty finding anything to eat without travelling back into Leverburgh. It wasn't far, but it was in the wrong direction. Perry approached two locals on the dockside.

'Morning. How we doing?' said Perry. There were a couple of nods back, but not much response. 'I'm DC Perry, over from Inverness, investigating the issues up at the Tides of Tranquillity.'

'I said that place would bring nothing but trouble.' The man who was speaking was square set, and Perry thought he looked like he could haul in ropes on his own.

'Why'd you say that?' asked Perry.

'Well, it's all strange, isn't it? They come in and it's almost like Fort Knox. You don't get in to see it. Yes, there's a couple of people work there, and those that do say it's all strange, all very highfalutin, you know. People coming in there, movie stars, they're different. People like that, all having their troubles. I think there are drugs going on. I think a lot of them are trying to come off them. This is where they keep them. Keep them out of the way.'

'You never see anyone from there then,' clarified Perry.

'Not really. My wife sees one of them. Down at the badminton club. Red-haired Irish girl. Says she's all right.'

The man behind him tapped him on the shoulder. 'She says that so you don't go down and see her. I've seen her. She's more than all right.'

'You talk to her at all?' asked Perry.

'As if. Like she's going to talk to me.'

'Don't see any of the others about?'

'Not really. The thing is, nobody supplies into it. Everything for that centre comes from outside. So it's brought in by truck. Ian works for them. Over there, that's him. Got a job with the hauliers. He's part-time, but he's run stuff in. You might want to talk to him. He's over by the creels.'

Perry turned away, thanking the men, and looked to see a bald man. He was indeed carrying creels out to a small boat.

'Would you be Ian?' asked Perry.

'Aye. Who would you be?'

'DC Perry. I was wondering if I could trouble you.'

'What's it about?' said the man. 'I haven't done anything wrong.'

'No, you haven't,' said Perry. 'You've probably heard there's been a bit of trouble up at the Tides of Tranquillity.'

'The foreign spa place.'

'Yes, the lads over there said that you run some of the lorries into there occasionally, their deliveries.'

'Occasionally? Well, I don't work full time for them. Not the whole year. I just pick up shifts here and there.'

'So you ship the goods in. Tell me how that works?'

'That's all that goes in, what we send by truck. Everything gets sent up to the depot in Stornoway, and we take it down. Often it comes over on a ferry, or sometimes they fly it in, depending on the weight of it. It all goes on to the one wagon dictated by the boss. And then I drive it in. So, all the basic needs, any additions, anything comes that way. Really don't want it coming from town, even if they are short. They ask for little that way, but in very rare cases they have to, it comes to us and put into our delivery. They are very funny about people seeing the interior.'

'Have you seen the interior?' asked Perry.

'I've seen the exterior. Didn't get to go inside. There's a road down the side that swings round to the back. You offload it there, but they take it inside. You don't see much.'

'How have you found them to deal with?'

'Well, they're a bit pernickety. Had to take a few things back because they weren't packaged up right or something or other. To be honest, I can't be bothered with them. They went and built that place, made a proper eyesore.'

'Okay,' said Perry, 'thank you.' He walked on around the dock until he saw someone parking up just beyond it. Perry wandered over and a woman got out.

'Hello,' said Perry, 'I'm wondering if I could trouble you.'

'I've just got this for Ian. He's about to go out. Give me a minute.' As the woman walked past Perry, she stopped and turned and looked at him. 'Who are you anyway?'

'DC Perry. If you could be quick and I'll have a chat with you afterwards.'

Perry watched as the woman ran over with a small lunchbox for the man he'd been speaking to earlier. When she came back, she almost straightened up to speak to him.

'How can I help you?' she asked politely, but she watched him like a hawk.

'I just wondered if you live local to here,' said Perry. 'There's been a bit of trouble up at the Tides of Tranquillity.'

'Oh, I heard about that,' she said. 'One dead, isn't there?'

'There is indeed one person deceased.'

'Murdered,' said the woman.

'We're investigating,' said Perry, not wishing to categorically say anything. 'I was just wondering; there was an Argentinian man who passed away. I wonder if you ever saw him out and about.'

'There was a man; he was slightly darker skinned than we are—walked about. But certainly English wasn't his first language. He would come past towards Leverburgh and cut by one of the houses.'

'Would you be able to point that house out?'

'Absolutely, you can't miss it because where he walked, that was the only one he went past. He didn't go near any of the other houses. I think he went past that one because, well, he's a young man, isn't he? There's a couple of young women in there. That might have been what it was about.'

Maybe he found himself a good time, thought Perry. *Living in that place all that time; well, younger guys, especially—they have needs. And not just cigarettes.*

'If you come now,' said the woman, 'I'm driving back that way. I'll point it out to you.'

'I've not got the car with me,' said Perry. 'The boss has it. I just wandered down here. You wouldn't mind taking me?

'Of course,' said the woman. 'Jump in.'

She ferried Perry round the corner and then stopped a little from a house that was further off into the moorland. At the rear, Perry could see a rather large hill, but it swept down to the front lawn of the house. He thanked the woman for giving him a lift and made his way over to the house.

As he entered through the front gate, he saw someone looking out the window. By the time he'd reached the front door, it was open. A blonde, thin woman, maybe in her early twenties, smiled at him.

'Hello, gorgeous. What can we do for you?'

'We?' said Perry. 'There only appears to be one of you there.' A red-headed woman, curvier than the first, stepped into the doorway from the side.

'We're both here if you can handle us,' said the woman.

Perry felt a little off balance. Women didn't talk to Perry like this. My goodness, he was old enough to be their dad.

'I was wondering if you could help me,' said Perry. 'I've got a question I'd like to ask.'

'Of course. Do you want to come in?'

It was quite cold outside and Perry had been walking about in the fresh air for most of the morning, talking to people. So, he agreed to go in.

'I'm Claire,' said the blonde woman. 'This is my friend Susan.'

'You lived here long?' said Perry.

'Well, we got the house . . . oh, when was it? Over a year ago. It was round about the time that the spa got built, according to the locals. We've only ever known it being there. It's having a bit of trouble at the moment, isn't it?' said Susan.

She showed Perry to a chair in the kitchen. As he sat down on it, she pulled another one up right beside him, and sat down so close that their knees were actually touching. She put her hand on his thigh.

'Have you come to ask about that?' she said. 'I don't mind you getting a little rough with me if I don't answer the questions.'

Perry felt awkward at this, but he also was confused. The women were flirting with him, and that didn't happen with Perry. Women did not flirt with Perry. His difficulty though was trying to work out why. He was a police officer. He was coming to ask questions. If you had nothing to hide, why would you flirt? He wasn't comfortable.

'I'm DC Warren Perry, by the way. Can you tell me if you got any visitors?'

'What do you mean, visitors? Like in the summer?' asked Claire.

'More sort of weekly locals.'

'That's a vicious rumour,' said Susan, slapping him on the back.

'I'm sorry, but I'm being quite serious,' said Perry.

'Well, the only person who came past the house, because we're at the end here, is Oswaldo,' said Claire. 'Oswaldo used to come past. He works up at the House of Tranquillity.'

'Worked,' said Perry. 'I'm afraid to say he's passed on.'

'He wasn't the . . .'

'The what?' asked Perry.

'The one wrapped in seaweed?' said Susan.

'How do you know about that?'

'One of the fishermen found the body, told his wife. I think we all know about it round here,' said Claire. She pulled her chair close as well. 'I liked Oswaldo dropping by. He was good looking,' said Claire. 'You don't get men of that calibre necessarily here. Younger lads going away. Off on the rigs or off on the boats, doing this and that. Bit of a shortage here at the moment. So it's good to see you.'

Perry knew they were flirting for some ulterior reason now! 'Did he ever say much to you, Oswaldo, when he came by?'

'Oh, he liked to do a bit of flirting. You know, he'd come in occasionally and have a coffee, but there was nothing in it. He used to tell Claire how her bum looked.' Claire stood up and gave her behind a little shake.

Perry stood up. 'Did he say anything else?'

'No, but come a minute,' said Claire, grabbing Perry by the arm. She took him out the back. He could see what looked like a solid curved roof greenhouse.

'What's that?' asked Perry.

'It's a polycrub.'

Perry looked at it. There was wood around the bottom, but the top was some sort of hard plastic. Almost like an Anderson shelter you could see inside.

'What am I looking at?' said Perry.

'That's our crub. We grow all sorts in here. Come on. Come in.'

Perry found himself being dragged again and spent the next ten minutes nodding simply as he had plants explained to him. Perry wasn't a green-fingered person. He wasn't someone that liked plants. If he wanted food, he bought it from the shop. He didn't grow it.

'Of course, there's not much at the moment,' said Susan. 'It's nice to be in here in the warm, isn't it? At least it's warmer than out there. Oswaldo used to come in here with us. I think he missed it, the heat, back in Argentina.'

'I thought they had quite-cool conditions at times as well. Depending where you were in the country,' said Perry.

'Well, he obviously must have been from the warm part, because that's what he liked. He liked it hot.' The two of them gave a titter. Perry wondered about the appropriateness of making a joke like that when someone was lying dead.

'Do you work?' said Perry.

'Not particularly. As little as I can,' said Claire.

'She's a lazy bitch,' said Susan. 'I work out here in the polycrub. Keep everything going.'

'So how did you come to get this place?'

'Rich friends,' said Claire. 'They helped us with it. And it's ours. It's a bit of excitement. The only problem up here, like I say, is there can be a lack of excitement.'

'I was going to say,' said Perry, 'don't take this the wrong way, but do you look like two girls who would enjoy a good time, like out at the clubs and that?'

Claire was tittering again. 'Kind of that obvious,' she said.

'That's not what he means,' said Susan. 'Yeah, well, we get up to Stornoway occasionally, but generally, we're here. I mean, this is life. This is what we signed up for. Bliss, isn't it? Perfect. A dream.'

Couldn't be that much of a dream for someone of her disposition, thought Perry. 'I best be getting back,' he said. 'Where do I walk, then?'

'Oswaldo came from round the side of that hill,' said Claire. 'Then he walked back round the other side.'

'What's the ground underneath like?'

'It'll be boggy at this time of year,' said Claire. 'You can try it, though, if you want.'

'Could you give me a lift round?' said Perry suddenly.

'Don't have a car. We get the bus if we want to go anywhere? It's a good life right here. Can't you see that?'

Perry nodded and thanked the women, taking his leave of them. As he exited the garden, he made for what he could see a small thin path stretching across the moor. Twenty steps in, he found the first bit of boggy land that nearly took his shoe off. He'd have to be more careful as he went round. The shoes he was wearing were not ideal. But that was the thing, wasn't it? He wouldn't have got away with wearing boots the way Hope did. Hers were practical boots, though, not stylish. But Perry sometimes wished he had boots of his own.

As he walked clear of the house, he wondered how the women afforded it. *I must visit the local letting agents*, he thought. *Let's see what it is about these women, and whether or not any of the estate agents will know how they afforded this house. I must check that through.'* He took another step forward. Perry heard the squelch before he felt the cold seep into his feet.

'Bugger,' he said. 'Should have got the bus!'

Chapter 12

Hope stood in the entrance to the Tides of Tranquillity spa resort, awaiting Alasdair to once again show her to a guest. This time she was going to talk to Zara while Ross had excused himself, retiring to do some more background checks on the various guests. When Alasdair approached Hope, she was pondering the fact that Macleod had still not got down.

He'd been looking to speak to someone that morning, but she thought she would have heard from him, telling her he was on the plane making his way over. All she had was an email. She thought she could do with him at the moment to give another perspective. Things were so quiet that it was difficult to make a start. So, anything that Macleod could offer would be appreciated.

'Miss El-Amin will see you now,' said Alasdair, and Hope followed the muscular, bald man along the corridor down to yet more guest quarters. It opened up into a very similar suite that she'd been in with Celeste. Everything you could want there, all your needs at your fingertips.

'Miss El-Amin, I have Detective Inspector Hope McGrath to speak to you.' There was a nod from the Middle Eastern woman. Hope realised that she really was quite petite. Hope was six feet tall and Zara El-Amin was five foot two at best. The inspector walked over towards her, but tried not to lean forward too much, so as not to loom over her.

'Thank you for seeing me,' said Hope. 'I'll try to be as brief as possible. It's obviously an upsetting time.'

Zara seemed a little shaken.

'Won't you have a seat?' asked Hope. 'It'll be easier for us to talk that way.' The young woman simply nodded, walked round, and plonked herself in the middle of the sofa. Hope found a chair opposite.

'How long have you been here?' asked Hope. The woman looked away for a moment before looking back. 'I asked how long you've been here?' said Hope. Again, the woman turned this way and that. Hope wondered if she actually spoke English.

Eventually, she said, 'A couple of weeks.'

'There are rumours you're over here because you need detoxing or to get off some sort of addiction. Is that correct?'

The woman said nothing, simply looking towards her feet.

'You need to talk to me,' said Hope. 'It's quite important that you do. Just so I can rule you out of the case. At the moment, everyone's under suspicion. But you're young. You're unlikely to deal with the pressure, well, as well as someone more experienced, such as Celeste. So I need everything you can give me just to clear you from the picture.'

'I'm here because my father sent me here. In my country, you don't refuse.'

Blimey, thought Hope. *He sounds like a bundle of fun.* 'On the night Oswaldo died, where were you?' asked Hope. The girl showed with her hands that she was in this room. 'Doing what?' asked Hope.

'Meditating,' said the girl. She reached forward and pulled a mat out from underneath the sofa. Putting it on the floor, she knelt down, and indeed, seemed to be meditating. However, she put it away again after ten seconds. Clearly she just wanted to demonstrate to Hope where she'd been and what she'd done.

'I was wondering, how do you get on with the rest of the guests?' The woman gave a little shake of the head.

'Can you articulate that? Add to it?' asked Hope.

There was a shake of the head. Certainly not

'Have you had any problems since you've been here? Any type of withdrawal or that? You seem very on edge,' said Hope.

The woman nodded very briefly. 'I'm getting treatment,' she said.

'What did you make of Oswaldo?'

'I got on well with Oswaldo,' said the woman. 'Very well.' Everything was so staccato, so basic in the answers. She didn't want to talk. Or did she not converse properly? No?

Hope stood up and made her way over to the window. 'It's quite the view from here. Do you feel out of touch? Do you feel that you've been banished?'

'I will not discuss my father's business with you. If you have business for here, I will discuss it, but not my father's.'

Wow, thought Hope, *for someone that was so reluctant to talk, as soon as we get into anything serious about family, she pulls down the blinds.*

'When are you heading back home?'

'Whenever my treatment's done,' said Zara.

'Well, I'll let you get back to it,' said Hope. Hope turned away, and walked back up the corridor, out of the front door, and sat down for a moment. This was getting difficult. If suspects didn't talk, you had to find out things about them. She hoped Ross would dig up enough to get them talking in the first place. However, that was still going to be a few hours away.

Hope took ten minutes, breathing in the salt air, letting herself relax. As she did so, a tingling sensation came again, that feeling of something in there. She walked back in and asked Alasdair to take her to Edward Pembroke.

At Edward Pembroke's door, Alasdair stood knocking for a long time. 'Sir Edward, I have the detective inspector for you.'

Hope realised that there was a peephole in the door. She hadn't thought about it on the other doors because they had been opened so readily and quickly. There was a sound as the door was unlocked. Hope thought someone had looked through the peephole. The door opened slowly. Once a man-sized gap was there, Alasdair walked through and someone almost jumped on him before stopping.

'It's you,' said Edward, coming into Hope's view. 'Do you not remember what I discussed with you? How to—'

'I introduced myself nice and loudly,' said Alasdair. 'I apologise if it wasn't enough.'

'I'll talk to the detective inspector now. Maybe she can help me.'

'Of course,' said Alasdair, and left.

'Come in. Come in, dear lady,' Sir Edward said to Hope.

He guided her round to one sofa that looked extremely similar to the other suites, but he sat beside her. He was once again wearing a waistcoat and jacket.

'Are you okay?' asked Hope, staring at Sir Edward. He was an older man, yes, but the smile he had shown yesterday was gone. There were worry lines across his face. He looked as if he hadn't slept. His hair was unkempt, and yet he still had a suit on.

'You have to keep watch for them,' he blurted. He walked over and lifted several items, then put them back down on the table. He checked the fruit bowl. Then he turned and looked at Hope. 'You don't mind if I ask you to stand and frisk you?'

'Excuse me?'

'You don't mind if I ask if I can frisk you? It's nothing sexual,' he said quickly. Hope shrugged her shoulders, stood up, let her arms go wide, and let her legs take up a slightly wider stance than normal. Edward patted her down professionally and in no way beyond what was required to check for any concealed items. After a minute, he stopped and looked up at her.

'I apologise for that, Detective Inspector, but you cannot be too careful when you've been in my line of work.' He walked across and pulled the blinds. 'They're all around, you know. All around. It's hard to detect. Someone like yourself probably wouldn't see them.'

'And are they here?' asked Hope.

'They're always here. Have you ever worked with people from my line?'

'I've met some from the Service,' said Hope, 'in the line of duty. They're very . . . well, you all seem to have your own agendas.'

'It's all agenda, isn't it? Maybe Oswaldo was the wrong man. Did they get the wrong one. Maybe they were coming for me.'

'Why would they be coming for you?' asked Hope.

'Can't say. I can't say things like that; you just have to take it—that's what it is. Not allowed to talk about things from then; got to be careful.'

'I heard you were no longer in the Service. You'd stepped out and were following your own pursuits.' Hope had read a brief email report from Macleod that morning, when he'd said he'd spoken to someone. Sir Edward was ill.

'I did leave. I gave a lot of years of my life. You build up a lot of enemies. They're all around. They don't forget. That's what you have to understand. They don't forget.'

'And they're coming for you, are they? What have you done?' asked Hope.

'What have I done? Too much. Too much they didn't like. Good at my job, you see. That was the problem.' He spoke fast. Very fast, and clearly agitated. 'Have you spoken to anybody within the service?'

Hope shook her head.

'Where are you from?'

'I've come over from Inverness, with the murder squad there.'

'Kirsten,' he said. 'Did you ever work with Kirsten Stewart?'

'Yes. Back when she was a police officer.'

'And since?'

'No.' She didn't want to tell him she'd met Kirsten recently, when she'd popped by the office.

'So, she was still a police officer when you dealt with her?'

'She was on my team. I worked with her,' said Hope.

'Might send her after me. Might send someone else. If it's them. I don't know.' Suddenly he grabbed Hope. 'Shush,' he said. He pulled her down, strongly, to lie in front of the sofa.

'What's the matter?'

'Shush,' he said. 'Can you hear them outside?'

Hope crept on the floor around to the edge of the sofa. She looked up into the windows. 'Don't rise! Sniper bullet,' he said. 'You could get a sniper bullet. Don't like the window. Don't like the window.'

He jumped up suddenly, rather sprightly for a man of his age, and pulled all the rest of the blinds down. Then he turned back to Hope. 'Can't see. Wouldn't take a risk. Wouldn't take a risk because I'd know they were here if they missed. Understand that?'

'You seem to be a lot more agitated than you were last night,' said Hope.

'Last night. Last night I was, well, I was sedate. Sedated. Give me things. Give me things to cope. But they haven't this morning. I think they wanted me to speak to you. To answer you. Sometimes the medication, it switches me down too much.'

'I can see you're obviously not well.'

'I am well,' he said, 'I just need refining, but I see it all. I see what they're like.'

'You see what?' asked Hope.

'I am ex-Service. I'm able to watch, able to pick up. Oswaldo, he was one for the women. He liked Skye. Have you met Skye yet? I can see why he liked Skye; young man, young woman, the usual thing, testosterone running wild. Nice girl, but Maddy, you've met Maddy. Maddy showed you last night. She likes to be in charge. Maddy likes to, well, thinks she's attractive. Puts me off. Puts me right off,' said Edward suddenly.

He walked over to the fruit bowl again and lifted it up. He then reached up to the shelf and ran his hands underneath.

'They bug places. You've got to be careful what you say because they bug places. Maddy could be the plant. Maddy could be the one. Yes?' He was staring at Hope like he was asking a genuine question. And yet he was raving like a madman.

'I haven't decided who's the one yet,' said Hope. 'Looking at the possibilities, looking at the reasons. Once we get them all in, that's when we'll deal with it. We'll talk about who's who.'

'Look at Maddy. Look at Skye. They were both, I think, seeing him. Seeing Ozzy.'

'Is that what you called him?'

'What everyone called him. Not Oswaldo. Ozzy. He liked it. After Ozzy Ardiles. Argentinian footballer. You remember him? No, you won't. You're too young. Of course. Sorry. You're just a young pup. A tall young pup, but a young pup.'

Hope realised she wasn't actually interviewing the man. He was more just rambling at her. But maybe he was right with what he was saying.

'Talk to Maddy. Ask Maddy about what happened. Ask Skye about what happened.'

'Do you know something for definite?' asked Hope.

'No. I can read them. Do you read people? I read people. I'm reading you,' he said. Hope stopped for a moment. 'You're looking a little edgy. You're going through changes,' he said. 'You're changing. You're struggling with it and you're changing. I can tell by looking at you. You're thinking about yourself. You're interviewing me and you're thinking about yourself.'

Hope found herself just now thinking about what he was rambling about.

'Do you know,' he said, 'we teach you all this. Right at the start. Teach you all this. But don't look to me. I'm not well. I know I'm not well,' he said. 'Suddenly get moments. Clarity. But you are well, and you can keep going and find out.'

He suddenly sat down. 'I'm tired,' he said. 'I'm tired. It's all this constant, constant on-the-go, constant checking over your shoulder, constant . . .'

He certainly was giving the impression of being agitated. 'Where were you the night Oswaldo died?'

'Exhausted. Asleep. Exhausted.'

'I may be back,' said Hope. 'Until then, I want you to stay. And don't overdo it. You look like a man wound up too tight.'

'Gotta keep alert,' he said. 'They're everywhere. Trust me, everywhere.'

Hope left his room before standing in the corridor. What was he? A nutter? Or was he a man with a problem? He could see things. She knew Kirsten could see things. Macleod had said, in Italy, he'd seen a whole new side to Kirsten. Well, maybe this man knew what he was talking about. Even if he delivered it in the strangest of fashions. She had little else to go on. So maybe a love triangle was where to start.

Chapter 13

Hope was having an unfruitful day. She'd gone round the rest of the suspects, but everyone was tight-lipped. And when she'd gone to see Skye, the yoga meditation instructor, the woman had gone out. Hope wasn't impressed. But things were moving slowly, and at least everybody else was in the same place.

Hope also had a meeting that night at Rodel to go to. She decided that this would take priority. However, she couldn't run on empty, and so for the back end of the afternoon, having not been able to talk to Skye, she grabbed a couple of hours' sleep. Waking up later, Ross and Perry had gathered at the temporary accommodation. They set up a call, bringing Macleod online from Inverness.

'Can I just start the meeting,' said Hope, 'by asking what happened with you getting over here.'

'I got pulled into something. It's just one of the things that happen. I'll be over tomorrow. You're okay, aren't you? Nothing getting out of hand.'

'Well, the press haven't arrived yet, which frankly has stunned me.'

'That's not strictly true,' said Perry. 'There's been some local press. By local, I mean people from the island. Probably sent down to get the stories. But if they're getting them out, it'll be everywhere tomorrow. Expect them in droves.'

'I'll get there by then.'

'So where are we at?' asked Hope. 'What have you got for us, Perry?'

'Having spoken to the locals,' said Perry, 'one of the things I've found out is that Oswaldo used to take a walk, always the same route, and pass by one particular house. There are a couple of women in there. Young, quite flirtatious. Flirtatious enough to be playing with me. Now, brace yourself, Hope. I understand I'm not God's gift to women. You can disavow me of that if you wish. But these two were acting like, well, maybe I was.'

'And you're a police officer and they're doing that,' said Hope.

'It reminded me,' said Perry, 'of the spa. A false front. A sort of another way of behaving in the world. Like the world doesn't work that way. It works this TV way.'

'Give me their address,' said Ross. 'Maybe I can try to look into it.'

'Do you think he was dropping in?' asked Hope. 'You know, maybe that was where he got his frustrations dealt with.'

'Can we just say sexual intercourse?' said Macleod suddenly. 'There's no need to dance around the issue. It is what it is. The guy's working in a spa. He's away from whoever, wherever, living there. Maybe this is what he does. Maybe he's even paying them.'

'That's a bit forward thinking for you, Seoras, isn't it?'

'I have seen a few things in my time,' he said. You don't have to hold back in front of me. It's good work, Perry, though. It's maybe worth looking at.'

'I'm going to go up to Stornoway tomorrow,' said Perry, 'to look at the estate agents. I want to find out who bought the house because, frankly, they don't look like they're capable of affording it. Places down in, what was it, Leverburgh, probably don't sell for that much. But they didn't look like they had anything. Also, they were like girls together. They weren't partners as far as I could make out.'

'Who else did you speak to?' asked Hope.

'Talked to a lot of the locals. Basically most of them are kind of fed up at this spa. It's plonked down and nobody particularly likes it. One, they see it as one not very Hebridean, and two, it's also not bringing in any of the revenue to the place. All the goods are delivered in from Stornoway and most of them are sourced from outside. It's a central haulage company in Stornoway that delivers, or rather does the last delivery of everything to them.'

'Some of the staff they have are local, aren't they?' said Hope.

'Minimal,' said Perry. 'It's minimal staff cleaning, and you've got the pool attendant Morrison. You've got the reception manager, Alasdair Ross, but in truth I mean he looks almost Hollywood, doesn't he? A cracking looking lad and he's on reception. So he fits in. They don't have anybody else, no one really . . .'

'Really what?' asked Macleod.

'Anybody ugly?' said Perry. 'I don't mean that disparagingly, but this is what I'm seeing. Everything about it is so TV, so Hollywood.'

'The beautiful people,' said Hope.

'Are we taking this a bit far?' said Ross. 'I mean, they're good-looking people. Maybe they just hired some decent-looking people.'

'No,' said Hope. 'They hired really good-looking people. When I talked to Saoirse, she was very aware of that.'

'Should I stay over here, then?' said Macleod. 'I mean, if it's the beautiful people, you can take charge, Hope.'

She slung him a look across the video call. 'You know I don't take kindly to being pointed out as that.'

'You can point it out to me if you want,' said Perry. 'After all, I'm getting a very different opinion of myself now with these two ladies in Leverburgh.'

'Back to the point, gentlemen,' said Hope. 'What else did you find out, Perry?'

'Like I say, everybody's kind of annoyed at it. But I can't find any of the locals who are going to do anything about it. They're going to grumble. They're going to say it shouldn't be done. But it's done and dusted. It's signed off. The building is there. It doesn't seem to have involved a lot of the locals. I think we need to look inside the building. We need to look at who's there. We need to look at who got it there.'

'Well, that's you, Ross,' said Hope. 'That's your side of things. Perry, you check up on these two women. What did you call them?'

'It was Claire and Susan.'

'Check the estate agents out. The women sound like possible contacts for Oswaldo, at least. Maybe somebody to go back to if we run out of steam of where we're going.'

'What did you find out, though, Hope?' asked Macleod.

'The ex-spy, Edward Pembroke, out of all of them who are here, apparently for treatment or to get better. He looks like a good guy.'

'That tallies with what Kirsten said to me,' said Macleod. There was silence.

'So, she's still about in Scotland?' said Hope.

'She is, and what she says here, and that she said it, doesn't go outside of this meeting. But I need you to understand where I got it from,' said Macleod.

'Can you fill me in on Kirsten again,' said Perry. 'She used to work for the team. That's right, isn't it? She's the woman you met in Italy.'

'Kirsten worked for the Service, Perry, but she's left it now. So, she's able to give me detail about the Service and be much more open than the current head, Anna Hunt, would be. At least she's our contact. I don't know if she is the actual head. I think she is.'

'What else did Kirsten say about him?' asked Hope.

'She said he was someone who looked into clinical advantage. That's how she put it. It's looking at decisive methods for gaining advantages for operatives out in the field. Kirsten didn't know exactly what he had looked into. But she said she could find out; however, that would upset the apple cart. This is why I'm saying don't say where I got any of this from and don't report it initially.'

'What sort of thing does clinical advantage cover?' asked Hope.

'That could be wide ranging,' said Perry. 'Think about it. If you want an advantage out in the field, as an operative, you could get drugged up. It could be gadgets. You could be maybe even benefit from languages, translator of customs, habits, being able to identify people remotely, there and then. There's so much involved in that.'

'So even like strength enhancers,' said Ross, 'stuff like that?'

'Well, that makes sense, but you could fit lots of stuff into that title,' said Perry.

'Whatever happened, he went a little nuts, paranoid, constantly seeing people about him,' said Macleod. 'So they retired him, but they monitor him. But they deemed he wasn't a particular threat.'

'That's quite something, isn't it?' said Hope.

'Well, maybe I'll clarify, Hope,' countered Macleod. 'He's not an active threat. He obviously knows stuff, so, therefore, that could be a threat. They're happy enough for him to go about, so they don't think he's going to do anything in whatever activity he's involved in. And those activities at the moment seem to be just trying to get better.'

'I also saw the boxer briefly today, Seoras. He's just angry all the time. I'm not convinced about him being a target, but he's very jittery. Very off the handle,' said Hope.

'Aren't all boxers like that?' said Ross.

'No,' said Perry. 'Quite often they're able to control their emotions, the great ones. Let it out in the right place, a boxing ring.'

'Is there anything,' asked Hope, 'from his past? I mean Oswaldo's. Anything come up yet, Ross?'

'I'm still searching through, but, to be honest, not a lot. He doesn't seem to have too much of a past. And that's kind of a problem.'

'Could it be you just haven't found it?' said Perry.

Ross threw him a glance. 'No, it's not there. A lot of it is not there. I don't understand why.'

'Has anybody offended Oswald?' asked Macleod. 'Has Oswaldo been in trouble with him? Was there any fracas?'

'The only thing that's been said to me,' said Hope, 'is that he might have been playing Maddy, the general manager, and the yoga and meditation instructor, Skye, off against each other.

The little I talked to Skye today, she didn't really mention it, seemed to poo-poo the idea that she was having any sort of relationship. Saoirse, I remember, when I spoke to her, said that Oswaldo came on to her, but she'd sort of laid down the law, and they then worked along fine.'

'And if he's got these women as well out in the house,' said Perry.

'So what,' said Macleod. 'He's romancing all these women, and somebody finds out that he's doing it, and then gets rid of him? He's wrapped up in seaweed as well. What's that about?'

'Saoirse has said to me it could be to cover-up needle marks. She said it's a possibility, although Jona said it's not proven.'

'Jona come back with anything yet?' asked Macleod.

'She's up doing autopsy in Stornoway. She's not come back with anything yet. It could be a while. You know what it's like when you're working away from the principal base,' said Hope. 'Anyway, I'm going to have to go soon. We're going to prepare for a meeting tonight.'

'We got a letter shoved through our front door, telling us to meet down at Rodel,' said Perry, staring at the writing. 'It's a church.'

'I know what it is,' said Macleod. 'It's well known by anybody on the island. At the end of the road, you can come round the back of the church. There are plenty of places you can stand and talk and not be observed down there.'

'Seems strange, though. I mean, we're here. They could just—' started Ross.

'Maybe it's somebody that doesn't want to talk out loud,' said Macleod. 'You're interviewing everybody in front of everyone. Or, at least, they know they're being interviewed. Maybe they want to tell you something on the quiet. Maybe they—'

'Hang on a minute,' said Hope. 'Edward said that he thought the room was bugged. Well, I thought that was just paranoia.'

'Paranoia is usually set off,' said Macleod, 'by something real. Whether what he's saying is real is another matter. But there's usually something behind it that causes the trigger.'

Hope reached down, suddenly, into her pocket and pulled out her phone. 'Give me a minute, guys,' she said. 'Just getting a call. It's from the centre.'

Hope answered the phone call. 'Inspector, it's Maddy here from the spa. I just wanted to say that I was doing my evening check of guests. Not like I check up on them, but I usually call round to make sure they've got everything they need, especially at the moment. And Jack's gone. He's not in his room; he's not in the spa at all.'

'Do you have a CCTV camera?'

'No,' said Maddy. 'We don't watch guests coming in and out. We don't want that. We keep it low-key because then people don't think that we have important people here.'

'Okay,' said Hope. 'I'll send someone over immediately.'

She put the phone down and looked up at the rest. 'Jack Harrison's gone missing from the spa. No idea how recent. Obviously, this evening. Maddy, the general manager, was walking around just to check and say hello to her guests and she said he's gone.'

'Get someone over there quickly,' said Macleod. 'I'll be over on the plane tomorrow and get myself down. Also, if you're going out to meet someone, if Jack Harrison's gone missing, make sure at least two of you go to Rodel.'

'Perry, you go to the spa. See what you can find out. Ross and I will go to Rodel and meet our contact. Once we've done that, we'll come and see you at the spa. Go through Harrison's room. See if you can pick anything up.'

'Will do,' said Perry. 'You can drop me off on the way, though. We could do with getting another car, to be honest. I'll pick one up tomorrow when I go up to Stornoway to the estate agents.'

'If you've got one, you can bring me down. There's no point running the locals ragged,' said Macleod. 'We can look after ourselves.'

'Come on, then,' said Hope. 'Let's get on to this. We'll see you tomorrow, Seoras.'

Hope closed the call, and soon the three of them were packed into the hire car, driving off to the spa. Hope dropped Perry off before driving along the winding road to where the church was at Rodel. There was a loop off the main road that went round the buildings at Rodel and Hope parked up near the main building.

In the darkness, it wasn't easy to see the grey walls. With the blustery wind and the light rain that was falling, the place looked foreboding. Hope had realised this coming out to the island. Whenever it was overcast, the place could seem quite bleak and yet when the sun shone, it was stunning. The sea was like that too. Cold and forbidding. And yet when the sun was on it, people wanted to swim.

She stepped out of her car, Ross following, and walked round the building. 'Can't see anyone,' said Ross.

'Now, let's not make ourselves too inconspicuous, though.'

Hope stepped forward in front of the building and saw an old grass-covered jetty heading out into the small sea lock in front of the main buildings.

'That's not the church, though, is it? The church is up there,' said Ross. 'Maybe we should be up at the church.'

'Maybe,' said Hope. But she was focusing now on an old quay.

'Do you know the Queen came along here once?' said Ross.

'Never mind that,' said Hope. 'Look, can you see something on that quay?'

Ross stared into the darkness. 'Yes,' he said.

Hope ran. The grass covering the old quay was wet, but she maintained her footing. She came across something lying there. As she drew up close, she could see it was a person. Hope whipped out her mobile phone, turning on the flashlight, and pointed it down. There, lying prone, his chest not rising or falling, was Alasdair Ross.

Chapter 14

It was the early hours of the morning when Hope drove through the gates of the Tides of Tranquillity. Perry had been there all night, and when she arrived, he looked bleary-eyed. She'd also been up all night with Jona, at first waiting for her to arrive, and also scouting the area to see if anyone else had been about. The area was extensive, after all. Though they had been asked to meet at the Rodel Church, she'd found Alasdair Ross down on the old quay.

Jona had come down through the night. Carefully, they'd divided off the scene, and it was still closed at this time. Hope had, however, been allowed to examine the body alongside Jona.

Alasdair Ross had been killed by some sort of heavy blow to the back of the head. 'Could it be a weapon?' 'Absolutely,' Jona had said. The possibility of a weapon was certainly likely. One of the other problems was, it was a heavy blow, but if you were strong enough, you could inflict it with your fists. She wouldn't know until she got the body back to the morgue and began further examination. She did, however, believe that the blow had been delivered more than once.

Hope took Perry to one side outside the entrance, and as she did so, she looked over, and could see a vehicle with a satellite dish on top. *They are here then*, she thought to herself. *Finally, the press had arrived.* This was the beginning of it. So far, it had been quiet. But now the local force would be stretched; trying to handle the press and keep them out of places they shouldn't be was difficult, and not something that she did.

'What have we got, Perry?' asked Hope.

'The other three guests say they haven't been out. I can't find anything to say that they have been. No CCTV, but they also were in the rooms. Now, Maddy said she'd seen them, but she saw them at a much earlier time. And then she was engaged with running around after Jack, trying to see where he'd gone. She didn't see the others after that, so she assumed they were in their rooms.'

Ross had been in the car with Hope, and now got out, coming up towards them. He looked over Hope's shoulder and pointed at her.

'What's up with our General Manager?'

Hope flashed a glance round and saw Maddy running out of the entrance up towards her. 'What's the problem, Miss Lyle?'

The woman's face looked worried, but she was tottering along on her high heels, unable to fully run. The skirt was also so tight that she couldn't walk at large strides, so she almost half-stuttered rather than ran.

'Ruairidh Morrison hasn't turned up today.'

'It's half six in the morning,' said Hope.

'Ruairidh Morrison was meant to be here at half five. I rang him last night, after Jack went missing. Told him to come in early, because I needed a break. I was meant to be covering the shift this morning. Ruairidh would come in later, and work towards the evening. But because of what happened, I said I'd probably be up, and I have been all night.'

Hope stared at the woman. It was clear, because the make-up wasn't looking as fresh as it should do.

'Are our three guests still where they should be?'

'They are,' said Maddy. 'I've just spoken to them.'

'Right. Where does Ruairidh live?'

'I've got an address for him. It's local,' said Maddy.

She turned on her heels, strutting back inside the centre, and Hope followed, Ross and Perry in tow. Once the address had been handed to Hope, she turned to Ross.

'Go see if he's at home.'

'He's not answering his phone,' said Maddy. 'I mean, he always answers to me. We pay him well.'

Hope didn't feel that this was good.

'What do you want me to do?' asked Perry.

'Are you still up for going up to Stornoway? Pick the boss up, but go through your estate agents before he gets in.'

'If I head off now, I'll be up there by half seven. None of them will be open.'

'No. Go and get yourself some breakfast. I'll hold the fort down here. If you find anything out, tell me. Otherwise, get back down with the DCI as soon as you can.' She looked over and saw a second vehicle pulling up behind the one with the satellite dish. 'They're really on their way,' she said.

'How'd they get over so early?' said Ross from behind her. A uniformed officer shouted. 'Nighttime ferry. Probably paid some money to get on.'

'Great,' said Hope. 'Just what we need. Go find me Ruairidh Morrison,' she said to Ross. And then she turned back to Maddie. 'I need to see the other three. I need to make sure they're okay.'

'Okay. Of course,' said Maddie. 'Follow me.' Hope, however,

knew the way to the rooms, so she kept stride with Maddy, finding it quite easy in her jeans and boots, as opposed to Maddy's high heels and skirt. As they got to the door of Celeste's room, Hope could hear someone shuffling about inside. Maddy knocked on the door.

'Hello, Miss Beaumont. I'm just checking up on you.'

'I'm fine,' she said, a voice inside, and then the door opened. Celeste was in her dressing gown and gave a smile. 'I've just been here. I'm fine.'

Hope nodded, and they moved on to the next room. The door opened before Maddy had even knocked on it.

'I heard somebody coming. I heard it. It's a good job, it's you. Is it true? Jack's gone missing. Somebody said Jack's gone missing.'

'It's true. At the moment, Jack is missing,' said Hope. 'And one of the staff, Alasdair, the man on the front desk, he's dead.'

Edward looked left and right suddenly. 'Are we safe? Are we safe?' he cried. 'I don't want to be a sitting duck. I don't want to be stuck in a place where I know they're coming for me. These people are good. You understand me? They're good.'

'Just wait in your room, please,' said Hope. The door shut abruptly. But Hope heard it open again when she started walking down the corridor. Edward looked out, up and down the corridor, before shutting it once more.

'It's a terrible affliction,' said Maddy. 'All these events have been bringing it on as well.'

'I think it happens all the time,' said Hope. 'I think it's more than just the events.'

Hope made her way to Zara's room, and she was found asleep in her bed. Maddy was reluctant to open the door, but given the circumstances, Hope needed to know that Zara was safe.

When they came back out to the front, she spoke to the local sergeant.

'I want somebody posted down at those rooms,' she said, 'until I get a handle on what's going on. We've got a killer abroad. It might be one of them, it might be somebody else.'

She walked to the front with Maddy and then told the woman to go on about her business. 'If possible, get some sleep.' But Maddy wouldn't leave the front desk unattended.

'Somebody has to be here for our guests,' she said. 'Our guests are the important thing.'

Maybe to her they were. Maybe that was her money. But for Hope, the important thing was now keeping everyone safe. She wondered how Ross was getting on with Ruairidh Morrison.

* * *

Ross had taken instruction from one of the local officers as to where Ruairidh Morrison's house was within Leverburgh. House numbers made little sense around these islands. Crofts were the order of the day. And Ross had learned from previous experience not to trust the satnav.

It was just after seven when he walked up to a small house in darkness. There were tufts of grass sticking up from an awkward-looking lawn. Ross wasn't sure if he would mow it or take out some hedge clippers and hope for the best as he cut it. He looked in through the open curtains. There was no attempt to have shut up for the night.

He went to go to the door and, pushing it, found it wasn't locked. There was an old-style handle on the front. In places like this, sometimes they didn't lock the doors and this would have a basic key lock. Ross opened the door. He announced himself.

'Mr Morrison. Ruairidh Morrison. This is the police. I'm Sergeant Ross. Are you in, Mr Morrison?'

There came no reply. Ross stepped into the hallway and flicked on the light switch. His eyes took a moment to adjust to what was a rather bland hall. Halfway down was a small coat area and sitting there was a Hoover. Taking a left, he stepped into a living room. It was basic, but had a Skybox and every other gadget going. There was certainly entertainment here, of the electronic nature. Ross noted that most of it was still on standby.

Ross made his way out into the kitchen at the rear of the house, and opened the fridge to find it reasonably stocked. There was a dishwasher. He opened that too and found several dirty plates inside. From there, Ross again called out for Ruairidh Morrison and made his way upstairs.

The bed hadn't been slept in as far as Ross could make out. He checked the other rooms and there was no one there. Trundling back down the stairs, Ross stepped outside into a rather bracing wind. Where would the man go? There was a small, not quite garage but more shed, area off to the side. Ross opened up the door to see a bike. There was a space on the shelf across from some tent pegs. So maybe the man had made off. Ross didn't know. The one thing was for sure, he wasn't here. He put a phone call in to Hope to advise her.

'To be honest, the house is empty. I don't think he slept here last night. I think he was on the run before that.'

'Is there any sign he planned to go away?'

'Well, the way the food is, and the way everything is, with the dishwasher, bed, lounge, it looks like he's not planned this for a long time. He's just gone. If you were going properly, you might even do your dishes. But no, nothing's been done. It looks like he's just legged it. I checked through some of the clothing upstairs as well. It doesn't look like there's a lot missing. But then again, I didn't know the full complement.'

'Should we organise a manhunt?' asked Hope.

'We could do,' said Ross. 'Probably wise, in case something's happened to him. The weather's not too good at the moment either. Why don't you get the Coastguard out, Mountain Rescue. Over here, it's a bit of a mixed bag, isn't it, when you go searching on these islands.'

'I will do,' said Hope, and Ross left her to organise. He returned to the car, and looked around. If the man was out in Leverburgh, he could be in any of these houses. If he had friends. Beyond that, where would he go?

Harris was connected to Lewis. You could go anywhere on the islands, both of them. You could drop by into little bothies that were out amongst the peats. There were plenty of old buildings, too. Maybe he had friends.

Some houses were not being used because it was winter. They were taken normally as summer lets. And you had lighthouses you could break into. You had many places. It was hard enough finding someone out here when they wanted to be found. But if they didn't, it would be immensely tough. But did it mean that Ruairidh Morrison had killed Alasdair?

That didn't seem to be right. There was no motive. Ross let out a deep breath and then sucked the air back in again. Usually, these places were a hotbed of gossip. Everyone knew everyone's business out here and yet with the spa, nobody seemed to know its business at all. Ross needed to get back into this. The trouble was, he was getting pulled here and there instead of onto his laptop. He drove back to the accommodation. On the way, he called Hope.

'Do you need me?' he asked.

'Kind of,' said Hope. 'It's just me here.'

'I want to get into the internet. Something's in there to find. At the moment, everything is so quiet round here. And now we've got this disappearing man.'

Maybe I could work on my laptop at the spa, thought Ross. Then again, who was I kidding. With Perry away to pick up Macleod, I wouldn't get to follow my own leads. I'd have to play second fiddle to what Hope was doing, there'd always be Jona to tap into as well, and a search on the go too. That should be Perry's to do.

But Hope was funny with Perry, Ross thought. She never treated him quite as a constable; often she trusted his intellect or his hunches. He didn't seem to do the same as someone like Susan Cunningham. Ross seemed to do a lot, but then again, he was better at the digging. Ross took a sigh. When Macleod was here, it would all be better.

Chapter 15

Perry drained the last of his coffee and looked at the two sausages in a roll in front of him. He pulled it back and slid open the packet of brown sauce before squeezing it and watching the viscous sauce drop over the sausages. Having assessed that there wasn't enough, he stood up, walked across the cafe, and found another packet. Bringing it back, he dumped a second load on his sausages.

Perry closed up the roll, took a bite, and chewed thoughtfully. Halfway through it, he realised it wasn't that easy to get through and he stood up to wander to the cafe serving bar to and ask for another coffee.

It was fifteen minutes later when he'd finished his sausage in the roll and his second coffee. Perry looked at his watch. Nine o'clock. Things would start to open now. Fortunately, the supermarket had been open, so he'd been able to get something although he'd had to wait for a while for the cafe.

Perry was getting that awkward feeling. Almost like he was drifting through the day without actually being there. He'd had little sleep. When he was young, it didn't matter to him. The adrenaline of the case set him off. Now, however, his routine of backing up vigour with cigarettes was gone. He'd have to replace it with something. Something was needed to get him going. He wasn't sure the coffee was doing the trick.

Perry hauled himself out to the car, drove into the centre of Stornoway, and parked up. Rather than pick out specific estate agents, he thought he would wander through. Most were tied in with solicitors. It took him the best part of an hour and a half to wander through each one. Most hadn't dealt with the case. He didn't find who had dealt with the house down in Leverburgh until he got to his penultimate destination.

He'd been counting them up as he went along, seeing ones across the road from the others, and he thought he had them all now in his sights.

Perry pushed open the door and almost half shambled in. The day was chilly outside and fatigue made it colder.

'Good morning,' said a bright voice on the other side. He turned to see a woman much younger than he, smiling across. She wore a long dress, smart and reserved enough for the office. Perry pulled back the chair in front of her desk to sit down. There was an awkward silence as he fumbled inside his jacket and then produced his credentials.

'I'm Detective Constable Perry, over from Inverness. I'm wondering if you could help me with a matter.'

'But, of course,' said the young woman, looking slightly perturbed.

'Your name is?'

'Taylor,' she said.

'After Taylor Swift?' said Perry, keen to show off his knowledge of current music trends.

'That's right,' said the girl. Perry stopped for a moment and looked at her. Taylor Swift wasn't on the go when she was born.

'You're telling me that your parents named you after Taylor Swift? Forgive me, but you're not old enough.'

'No, no, I call myself Taylor,' she said.

Perry tried to stop the frown growing on his face. It was one trend these days, wasn't it? They called themselves by their own name. What was wrong with what you were given? But he managed not to show his resentment and smiled as he looked at her.

'I don't know if you'll be able to help me. How long have you been here?'

'Six months,' said the girl.

'I'm looking into a house in Leverburgh,' said Perry, writing down the address on a pad of paper on the table. 'This is it. I want to see if the company dealt with it.'

'Just give me a moment.'

The woman turned to the computer on her desk. She punched away on the keys. Today they are something else, Perry thought. This is it. Next generation, they did this type of thing so effortlessly.

Computers came in late with Perry. They were very much still in development when he first got hold of them. And now, well, they did whatever. It was nuts what they could do. You got apps and such like on your phone. Far beyond what the old PCs of his day could do. Even the games. Games on your phone. TV on your phone. It was all nuts.

But they don't have our music, thought Perry. Was that a conceit? Was that just his way of stopping himself from getting older? Or pretending that things were always better? Perry thought about this. Things were never better or worse, were they? It was the same maelstrom, the same chaos that ran round and round. You just tried to look back with rose-tinted glasses to remember the good times, forget the bad ones. That's probably how you survived being a human.

'We did do that transaction. However, obviously, I wasn't here. Do you mind if I pop into the back for a moment? I'll just get Mr Anderson. He'll be able to help you better. He would have been here when the deal was done.'

'Splendid,' said Perry, and sat back in his chair. Mr Anderson came back and was a rather stocky man, but with small, round glasses. He sat down opposite and then leaned forward, peering at Perry.

'DC Perry from Inverness. Taylor said that you handled a transaction to buy this house.'

'Oh yes, not long over a year ago.'

'Do you remember the name?'

'Two young women bought it. I can look for them here. A Claire Jennings and a Susan Moffat,'

'That's right,' said Perry; 'so they bought the house.'

'It was bought for them. I remember distinctly. There was an uncle, I think. They came in and viewed the house. They were the ones we saw, but he paid for it.'

'Do you know his name?' asked Perry.

'No, not off the top of my head. Give me a moment.' The man went back into his computer. He turned back to Perry. 'Kyle Howarth.'

'Is there an address there for him?'

'There is. It's on the mainland. In fact, it's down in England.'

'Write it down for me, please,' said Perry. 'This uncle, did you ever speak to him?'

'Very briefly. It was to do with the money being passed over.'

'How did he behave towards his nieces?'

'To be honest,' said Anderson, 'I don't know if they were his nieces or not. They said he was their uncle. That's where the money came from. I didn't need to know that information. So, if I'm honest, I couldn't honestly tell you if he was their uncle or not. All I can say is that the transaction came from a man with that name living at that address and the money went into the account, no problem.'

'Well, thank you then,' said Perry.

He was quite happy because Macleod needed picking up in about forty minutes. He could get a coffee in before Macleod arrived. Macleod was a good boss, but when a case was on, he was all go. Perry wasn't like that. Perry actually liked to stop. Macleod would have his team running here, there, and everywhere. Perry needed time to rest. To chew things over.

The cigarettes had done that. Cigarettes were always a good excuse to get out. Stand and think. People thought he was just taking time off, but in truth, Perry did most of his best work away from people.

He drove the car up to the airport and sat having a coffee, waiting for Macleod's plane to get in. When it landed, he met the boss coming through the small doors into the baggage reclaim. At Stornoway Airport was a small conveyor which was usually quite crowded, even though most of the aircraft didn't hold more than fifty people. Perry had also picked up the second hire car and sat back in the seat as Macleod got into the passenger side.

'So what have you been up to then this morning?' asked Macleod.

'I've been going round the estate agents, like I said I would. Kyle Howarth paid for this house that Oswaldo used to visit on his walks with the two women. I've got an address for him. I was thinking of contacting some of the forces over there. See if they'll go and do a bit of work for us.'

Macleod looked at it. 'England. That's not far, that's not far outside Nottingham. That's where Susan is. Did you know she's got the prosthetic now? They're just keeping her there for a few days. Make sure everything's all right.'

'I haven't even spoken to her since a few days ago. Last night was just nuts.'

Macleod picked up his phone, and he called Susan Cunningham.

'How are things?' he asked.

'It's good, Seoras. It's going to take a wee while to get used to walking with it. I kind of got used to the crutches. I was a bit of an expert on them.'

'I remember,' said Macleod. 'Are you free?'

'Free? Why? What do you need?'

'I've got a house for you to visit.' He passed on the details of Kyle Howarth.

'I'll get a taxi out,' said Susan. 'That's no problem. I'm not needed here just now. Any trouble, is there? I'm not in the best condition, obviously. We kind of got blindsided last time. Weren't expecting it.'

'No, and don't take any risks. It's just a case of finding out who he is, what he's doing there, and why he bought a house. And does he have any nieces?'

'No problem, then,' said Susan. 'They're not wanting me back in the hospital until tomorrow? They said I should try to get about a bit. Obviously not push it too much. But if I get a taxi, that'll be fine.'

Macleod closed down the call and sat back.

'I don't mean to be forward, Seoras,' said Perry. 'But, well, do you think it's wise bringing her in at the moment? Just let her focus on the—'

'I gave her a choice,' said Macleod.

'Well, yes, and no. A choice from you is not always a choice, is it?'

'I don't force people to do stuff.'

'No,' said Perry. 'The personality does, your demeanour and your position. She'll want to do it for you, even if she isn't a hundred per cent.'

'Point taken,' said Macleod, looking out the window. 'But people have their own minds, like you. You could have said nothing, but you just did. Anyway, what's your take on this? Got another person dead now.'

'We're skimming the surface. We're skimming the surface because there's a complete show going on,' said Perry. 'I think the boss knows it too. All the guests, they're pretenders in some ways. All pretenders except for that guy from the Service. Edward. He's very messed up. Jittery. Jumpy. But I don't get that one. To be that bad and then be let go by the Service, not to be watching him.'

'He's probably going to be the most secure person in the service. If you're that paranoid, you'll be taking precautions like anything and you'll be telling nobody anything,' said Macleod. 'I perfectly get why they let him go.'

'Suppose,' said Perry. But his voice wasn't convinced.

As they drove down from Lewis into Harris, before heading for the east side of Harris, Macleod pointed out various lochs and mountains to Perry, especially the Clisham. Perry sat, not listening intently, but giving the appropriate nods. It was now he could see Macleod being almost reminiscent. When he worked with him in Glasgow, he was never that.

The man had changed. The man was, well, less resentful

inside. The mind was always there. It always had been. But now there was something different about him. Perry liked it, to be honest.

As they passed through Tarbert, heading out towards the Golden Road to route down to the Tides of Tranquillity, Macleod reached for his phone. It had been on vibrate, and Perry was impressed, because usually the man missed it. He wasn't the best with technology. He even made Perry look like an expert.

'Susan,' said Macleod, answering the phone. 'Really? Well, that's not that much of a shock, I guess. Well, thank you for doing that. It's much appreciated. And you say, never? Okay, excellent. Go get yourself sorted. I'll see you back up north when you're ready.'

'What was she saying?' said Perry as soon as the call was closed.

'She's been to the address and there's no one of that name there. There's no Kyle Howarth to talk to the neighbours. There never has been.'

'So someone posed as Kyle Howarth. Someone put these two women there. But why?' asked Perry.

'Should we go ask them?' said Macleod.

'I don't know,' said Perry. 'I guess we'll run that one past Hope, if that's all right with you.'

'It's Hope's investigation,' said Macleod. 'I was asking more for you to think it through with me.'

'Well, there's something up with it. We could barge in asking them about who we're missing. But they'll know we are on to them. We don't know what connection they have. Why they would want the house paid for? Who would put them there? We put the frighteners on and connections will sever. And the last thing they'll do is make those connections in the spotlight. If we let them continue, we might even catch them at it.'

'That's what I was thinking. We'll tell Hope. See what she says,' said Macleod.

Perry watched Macleod sit back in the chair, looking around him as Perry turned down the golden road. He couldn't watch him for too long because the road twisted and turned and Perry had to concentrate on his driving. Still, the big boss looked relaxed. This was always good news.

Chapter 16

Hope had only talked briefly to Skye Anderson, the Welsh yoga instructor. But now, having heard others accuse her of being in an affair with Oswaldo, she wanted to nail down what was going on. Skye had been absent on her last visit, but Hope was determined that this time she'd talk to her.

As she walked through to the front reception, there was no Alasdair Ross, but instead Maddy Lyle. She looked slightly flummoxed, despite maintaining a pristine blouse and skirt, as Hope approached her.

'Yes, Detective Inspector, how can I help? If you'll forgive me, it's quite chaotic at the moment. I feel like I've been up most of the night.'

'I have been up most of the night,' said Hope, and reached round to adjust her ponytail, as if to say so.

'Of course. What can I do for you?'

'Is Skye around?'

'She has come in this morning. She'll be down in her yoga suite. I think she was meant to be working with Jack this morning.'

'I'll find it,' said Hope, as Maddy went to lead her forward.

Maddy went to continue anyway, but Hope said once again, 'I'll find it.'

As Hope walked along, she wondered if Ross would come up with something. He'd gone back into looking on his computer. It's always better when you let Ross get on the internet and start digging things up. Macleod would be here soon, and if she needed backup beside her, she'd have Perry or Macleod. But for the moment, she was on her own.

She saw the sign on the door saying yoga and meditation, gave it a quick rap, and then on hearing 'come in,' she opened it. Sitting in the middle of the floor was Skye Anderson. If you were making a TV program, Skye would be the yoga instructor. She was young, looked supple, and had long black hair. It ran well past her shoulders.

It wasn't tied up in a ponytail like Hope's hair. Hope was being practical, although she liked her hair out. But when you were working, it got in the way. Skye, however, seemed to always have her hair out on the few occasions that Hope had seen her.

She was sitting cross-legged on a mat on the floor. Skye had on black trousers and a black crop top. She probably wouldn't have looked too out of place if she'd gone out clubbing. If there were sheiks and wealthy businessmen coming over, Hope could see that Skye was the meditation specialist that they would look for. But Hope was also of the belief that though Skye was the meditation specialist that they would look for, she could probably do the job.

That was the thing about everyone here. Maddy had picked people who could do the job, not simply just look gorgeous. That wasn't always easy to come by but Hope guessed with the right money, it could be done.

'Detective Inspector,' said Skye.

'I'm sorry I've interrupted you,' said Hope. 'If you've got a moment.'

'Of course,' said Skye, almost leaping up to her feet.

'I need to talk to you,' said Hope. 'You're probably aware by now there's been another death. Alasdair Ross is dead. Jack Harrison is somewhere. We don't know where.'

'Well, I don't know.'

'Ruairidh Morrison hasn't come in for work.'

'I did hear. In truth, I had thought about legging it myself. But I thought this might be the safest place. To be at my place of work. To be about where there's plenty of people. You've also got your people about.'

That is true, thought Hope. *There are uniform around. This could actually be the safest place.* 'Several people have told me you were having a relationship with Oswaldo.'

'A relationship?' said Skye. 'I guess it would look like that. Ozzie and me. Well . . . we were stuck here. There's no one really to . . . how would you put it?'

'I don't know,' said Hope. 'You put it for me.'

'Some of us are very physical. I may be someone looking at the mind and about the soul, but the physical comes with that as well. Oswaldo was a man who needed his women, so to speak. We used each other for sex, or rather we enjoyed each other for sex.'

'That's very forward of you,' said Hope.

'Well,' said Skye, 'it's just me. I'm usually in a relationship with someone. I have been since I was about eighteen. Not always serious, if you'll understand. But this girl needs certain things at certain times and Oswaldo was more than happy to oblige and, to be honest, we got on reasonably well together for what we did.'

'Did you spend any other time together?' asked Hope. 'Did you know him well?'

'I would be able to describe his physical body rather than his mental attitude or what was going on in his life,' said Skye. 'Similarly, he probably couldn't tell you anything about me other than my measurements and shape.' She laughed a little, then her eyes darkened.

'I was shocked when he died. Ozzy got a few people's backs up, I guess. I haven't been looking for any men around here. What I did with Ozzy, I was doing on a quiet basis. Of course, people would see him come to my quarters and we'd meet occasionally. But because sex was all it was, we weren't running around together. And I didn't make a big show of it. Why bother?'

'I heard that Maddy, you, and Oswaldo were caught up in a bit of trouble together. A bit of a triangle going on.'

'Seriously?' Skye said. 'Maddy is super focused on the job. But she was always super focused on Oswaldo. The thing about them, those two, was that Maddy needed Oswaldo for what skills he was bringing to the spa. But he was sloppy.

'I get my job done. She never complained about me. My clients turn around and say I do things well. But Maddy was a little jealous because I'm younger than her. She has a beauty, Maddy,' said Skye, 'and not just a figure. She's clever and determined. And yes, she's got a splendid figure for her age. All in all, she's a very attractive woman, but a woman who suffers because she's worried about the others around her. I'm no threat to her, for any man. Oswaldo, however, played her.'

'In what way?' asked Hope.

'There were a few irregularities going on. I don't know

exactly what. I never asked him. Never needed to. But Maddy and him had a bit of a fracas. But he played her to keep his position. She wanted him. Younger man. I mean, he was attractive. Very attractive. Very engaging. And for someone like Maddy, he was someone to be captured. Not conquered. Conquered is too much of a word. Maddy wouldn't conquer him. Maddy would want him. Longer term.

'But she, to Oswaldo, was the boss that needed sorting out. Needed to be played when he wasn't doing what he should be doing. Whatever that was. I'm sorry,' said Skye. Skye turned away and Hope watched her stretch her arms out before turning back. 'It's all been a little . . . well . . . am I safe here?'

'I don't know,' said Hope. 'We're keeping the place as safe as we can, but I don't know what's going on yet. And if I do find out, you'll be safer. So, make sure you tell me everything.'

'Of course,' said Skye.

'These irregularities, can you think of what it was about? The ones that Oswaldo would have been keeping Maddy sweet about.'

'It was something to do with Ozzy's treatments,' said Skye.

'What sort of treatments does Ozzy do?' asked Hope.

'I don't know. Maddy's a stickler. Maddy likes all the paperwork in place and Maddy likes the clients looked after. If you do that, Maddy is happy. She never gave me grief and trouble because I did my job, and all my paperwork was in on time. So the fact that I was in bed with Oswaldo might have annoyed her, but it didn't take her away from what her main focus always is. Running this place and keeping it ship shape.

'But Ozzy was slack with his paperwork and his clients. I never asked him. I never found it out from him. But I think he bedded Maddy to keep his position. I think he played her all along to try to make sure he stayed here.'

'And you felt nothing about that. You were okay if he did that.'

'I told you. Oswaldo and I, it was like going to the gym. Now some people don't get that. Some people see sex as more than that. It can be for me but that needs a special kind of sex and a special guy. Ozzy wasn't that special kind of guy. Ozzy was just someone hitting a need for me, and I was hitting a need for him. Will I miss him? Honestly, not particularly. I don't think he was good for the place. Maddy's obsession with him and if he was sleeping with her to sort out the job, that's not good. Do you get me?' said Skye.

'Are you happy here?' asked Hope. 'I mean, is this your dream job?'

'Of course it's not. We don't get out of here. I talked to Saoirse about this. You know, because there's not that many of us girls here. Maddy, you can't speak to in that way. She's the boss. Saoirse, like myself, finds herself at loose ends at times.'

'What do you do?'

'It's funny when you go away with your time off, but here, we're kind of restricted in. We're not part of the community. They don't want us here—a lot of them—and I don't blame them for that. I mean, look at it. Why is this here? This is a playground for people with money. Every time I get someone come in to look at me, the first thing they say is, in their heads, did she get this job because of how she looks?'

'Did you?' asked Hope.

'Did you?' Skye asked back.

'Well, you may find that out, as this case goes on,' said Hope with a smile. 'But did you?'

'Yes, I got it because of my looks. But I can do this job, and I have done this job for a while. There were others in for it. I knew some of them. They were as good as me. One of them, a woman called Angela. She was like you. A good-looking woman. And she had a scar like you have.'

Hope resisted the urge to reach up and touch the scar from the acid that had been thrown at her when she defended Macleod's partner. It was a war wound she was proud of. But she was a woman. And in some people's eyes, it diminished her looks. The people that mattered didn't see it that way.

'What's your long-term goal?' asked Hope.

'I'm building up some money. I'll have my own practice. A couple of years. Saoirse's the same. Did she tell you that?'

'She did.'

'You must find it strange here. Have you ever worked in this sort of type of world?'

'What world are you talking about?' asked Hope.

'People come in here with silly amounts of money. You bend to their every whim, to a point,' she said, suddenly putting her finger up. 'I don't bend that way for them. I do a job for them. Yes, I might dress as they would like me to dress. And some of them clearly enjoy the fact that they have a young healer, as they would put it, before them. And I play on that, but I don't go any further.

'But this place is, well, we're not frauds. But for the money they're paying, they want more than healing. They want to be through an experience. They want to think they've got something more than what anybody else has got. And that's where Maddy's so good with them. That's why she's here. Myself, Saoirse, Oswaldo, we're here because we look good. And Maddy can use us to provide that experience.'

Hope thanked the woman and turned away, but Skye

shouted after her. 'What happened?' she asked. 'Forgive me, but what happened? With your scar?'

'I protected the boss's wife. Stopped her from being dumped in a bath full of acid.'

'It's beautiful.' Skye said to her. 'Do you know that? It's beautiful.' Hope turned to walk out the door. She then thought, *Is Skye playing me?* Everything Skye said made sense, but Hope was very like her at one point.

Hope had been in that position of being always looked at and admired for not her skills, but for her looks. Hope could be the beautiful detective, or at least could have been. Not anymore. She could be the heroic one on TV now. Not the stunning one, not the pristine one. She laughed at herself. But she suddenly realised that was the truth of this place, wasn't it? Or at least, that's what it was meant to be. She looked up to see Ross marching down the corridor.

'Hey,' said Hope. 'What's up?'

'The Tides of Tranquillity have a board overseeing them. It's occurred to me,' said Ross, 'we've got Maddy here. We've then got a board. We need to get to know what their goals are. Is it simply to make money?'

'Ultimately, that's what everybody wants to do, isn't it?' said Hope. 'Ultimately. But why here? Why away? Why so secret?'

'Because then you get the celebrities.'

'But as a board, is that really what you want to be doing? You just want to make the place run. You could make it bigger. But they've gone for one particular place. We need to understand why this place was built. Because at the moment we seem to be skimming the surface, not getting in behind it, seeing if there was any conflict within the group, more so than with the locals.'

'There's definitely conflict with the locals,' said Ross, 'but it doesn't seem to be a local thing. That's the problem.'

'We've got one of them dead. We've got a healer dead. I've also just been told that there were issues with what Oswaldo was doing. Paperwork issues. He may also have been sleeping with Maddy,' said Hope. 'The trouble is, I don't have any evidence about what was going on with the locals. I don't have any of this. Not a soul. I can definitely get with what they're saying.'

'Jack still hasn't turned up,' said Ross. 'I think it's time to call for the manhunt proper.'

'Well, Macleod's on his way. We'll pull everybody in together as soon as he's here. Talk through our operations.'

Chapter 17

'So, these are the digs then,' said Macleod. 'Which room's mine?'

'There's a small bedroom up at the back,' said Hope. 'Either that or you're going to have to find a hotel.'

'You're giving me the small one,' said Macleod, his eyes piercing. He continued to hold the stare for a moment and then burst out laughing. 'That's fine,' he said. 'We better get down to proper matters.' He dropped his small suitcase in the hallway and walked through to the lounge. Perry had moved the dining room table into the lounge. There were bits of paper here, there, and everywhere, and Ross had his computer set up.

'We had worked out of some offices in Tides of Tranquillity, but to be honest, we need somewhere well away,' said Hope. 'Not happy talking in there now. I don't understand what's going on, and somebody is clearly up to something.'

Macleod sat down, and Hope joined him before Ross came through from outside.

'Good to see you, sir,' said Ross.

'Where are we at?' asked Macleod.

'Well,' said Hope, 'there's a myriad of motives going on and

I'm struggling to pull out the threads, Seoras. If we take it from the top, we have the death of Oswaldo. Oswaldo is one of their healers, one of their alternative therapy operators. He stays on site, the same as Saoirse and Skye, living on the premises, brought in because they look good as well as being able to do their job. You have Maddy, who's running the place, and who's setting up the whole image and maintaining it. A stickler, apparently, for the treatment it's given, but also for the experience the guests get. Skye was having sex with Oswaldo.'

'So, she was having a relationship,' said Macleod.

'No, she was not. She was having sex with Oswaldo. It was not a relationship; it was a purely physical thing. She was adamant about that.'

'Okay,' said Macleod. 'That's never worked for me.'

'Rather than get into the detail of your love life,' said Hope, 'trust me that for some women, and probably some men, it can work like this. However, we believe that Maddy actually liked Oswaldo. Oswaldo, however, was not producing the correct paperwork for Maddy for his treatments, according to Skye. Therefore, she believed he was bedding Maddy to keep his job.

'Meanwhile, we've got four guests. One of whom, Jack Harrison—the boxer—has run off. We've got a Service spy who's losing it big time. We've got an actress who wants to be back to her best physically, and needing help with that. And we've got a little scared girl from the Middle East. At least, that's what she feels like to me. By the looks of it, Daddy's put her here, or whoever else looks after her.

'We've also got one local dead—Alasdair Ross. He's the reception manager. So like Maddy, he would be involved with a lot of the running of the place. So he might have known what's going on. We've also got missing at the moment, one

Ruairidh Morrison, a pool and sauna attendant. He's a very minor figure in some ways and yet, he's suddenly shot off. Just disappeared. A lot of people are afraid though,' said Hope. 'I know that Skye thought about running it.'

'On top of this,' said Perry, 'we've got this house that was financed by an uncle of the two women in there. But he doesn't exist even though he paid from an address that he's never been at.'

'That account's now closed as well,' said Ross. 'I'm trying to chase back through, but it's a nightmare. Can't get anywhere to see who really set it up.'

'I don't know what you wanted to do with that house, whether you wanted to let them continue out there. If we raid and we go hard,' said Macleod, 'those two women could leg it or whoever's making the contact could leg it.'

'But we know Oswaldo went there,' said Hope. 'That's the key to me. He's doing a walk. He doesn't interact with anybody else in Leverburgh. Unlike Saoirse, who's out, amongst the locals.'

'Skye's not out amongst the locals, though, is she?' said Perry.

'Skye's the opposite. Skye stays there. Skye's social life is Saoirse, according to her,' said Hope.

'As I see it,' said Macleod, 'Jack and Ruairidh are prime suspects at the moment for the murder of Alasdair. Jack's been described as a loose cannon. He hit Perry. Maybe something wasn't right. You've got the local connection between Ruairidh and Alasdair. Maybe something's been said; maybe Jack's been pulled into that. Has Jona come back yet, with any further detail about what could have caused Alasdair's death other than a heavy object in the back of the head?'

'She can't tell if it was fists from a properly trained fighter—

hard fists—or whether it was just a solid implement,' said Hope. 'It's all a bit chaotic, isn't it? Trying to look for one thread through, and we're not finding it. Why does Ozzy get killed? Maddy could have a motive. If he's sleeping with her, using her just simply to keep his job, and she finds out and she understands that she's a woman scorned, she could kill him.

'Is Skye covering up? Or if she has something for him, and she's not happy, and he then beds Maddy, well, she's got a motive. She says he didn't interest her, but if she did it, and he had been interested in her, or things had been going on, she's going to keep as clear as possible.

'We've got our paranoid spy. Has he gone off and done something? Has he mistakenly thought Oswaldo was coming after him? Alasdair too.'

'I can't see how Celeste is involved. Nor the princess,' said Perry.

'Need to find Jack,' said Hope. 'We have had little conversation with him, other than when he got violent. We need to find him quickly. He might end up like Ozzy and Alasdair? But the deaths are very different. One wrapped up with seaweed. And then with the second, there's no attempt to cover up. So we need to find him.'

'The manhunt's been put together,' said Perry. 'I've got the teams out, but we have found nothing yet.'

'I'm going to interview Maddy,' said Hope, 'as soon as we get away from here. However, I'd like to know more about what sort of person Alasdair was.'

'Well, when I've been talking to the locals,' said Perry, 'they've come back and said Alasdair was always a decent man. Fair. Conscientious. He was a looker, obviously. He was someone who could keep his head. Someone who would know how to play things.'

'And that's maybe why he was meeting you outside. Away from everything,' said Macleod. 'If Alasdair knew something was up, maybe he didn't want to be seen talking to you.'

'He'd organised this house,' said Perry suddenly, 'so he would know we were here. He would know to put the letter in. With being on reception, he saw us come and go. He knows what we're doing to a large degree. So, it made sense that it was a letter from him,' said Perry.

'But somebody obviously followed him. Somebody knew he was there. Somebody killed him. But they've left him down, not at the church where he was to meet us, but further down,' said Hope.

'Did Jona say the body was moved down to there?' asked Macleod.

'No,' said Hope. 'When I spoke to her last, she didn't say that. She never indicated that the body was moved to be placed down on that quay.'

'Interesting,' said Macleod. 'Must have been intercepted. Alasdair must have known who he was talking to.'

'But he'd have known them all,' said Hope.

'Exactly, and he'd have known Jack,' said Macleod. 'Did he run? Is that why? Did he have to run from the church, and he was found down there?'

'Forensic has mentioned no signs of a struggle, in that sense,' said Hope.

'Was Alasdair then talking to someone? Was someone engaged with him? Conscientious man. Maybe, one of the guests was out and about and he wanted to bring them back. He was worried about them. Maybe it was another local. Maybe it was Ruairidh talking to him. Ruairidh wanted to talk about something. Maybe Alasdair didn't want that to go to you, so he moved down to the quay,' said Macleod.

'There's too many possibilities, Seoras, at the moment,' said Hope, frustrated. 'Too many.'

'There is,' said Macleod, 'there is . . .'

'Can you excuse me a minute,' said Perry. He stood up and walked out of the room, and Hope heard the front door opening. Macleod looked over at Hope.

'What's he doing?' asked Hope.

'He always pops out every now and again,' said Ross.

'Not in the middle of a meeting,' said Hope.

'His phone didn't go off, did it?' said Ross.

'No. It didn't.'

'When we were in Glasgow, we used to do this. I'd say he was going out for a cigarette,' said Macleod.

'You think he's back on them,' said Hope. 'Haven't smelt them.'

'No, he's doing what he used to do. He's off to think.'

Hope nodded, asked to be excused, and walked from the room. She opened the front door, stepped outside and looked to see Perry standing at the end of the house, looking out, towards the sea.

'What's up?' said Hope.

'Thinking,' said Perry. 'I'm thinking. I'm trying to tie these thoughts all together. I'm trying to put together how this fits. And I can't. It's like a scramble,' he said. 'There are stories, but there isn't a complete tale. What do we know about all these people? Just that several of them are fabulous and here for treatment. Not unwell, but getting treatment. No links to the local community.

'The local guys. Decent. Not seen as a problem. A few people are sleeping with each other, but that's not a big issue. Jack Harrison, up in arms. Why? Oh, he's just an eggy boxer. Our spy could be an issue. Why? Because of his illness. And then you have that one suspect that it can't be,' said Perry. 'The one perfect suspect it can't be. Like everything is covered up so well, all the suspicions thrown at everyone else except for that one person.'

'You think it's her?' said Hope suddenly.

'No,' said Perry, 'not for a minute. She's a scared woman. She's here against her will. But she will not kick up a fuss. And in some ways that looks good. Because she's that perfect suspect. What I'm saying is there's a story being written here. There's a story written for us coming in.

'Think about it. Somebody got rid of Ozzy. Wrapped him in the seaweed and put him into the sea. If he ever surfaces, the needle marks are gone. Otherwise, why bother wrapping him up and dumping him? Just get out of there!'

Perry stamped up and down, now beginning to feel the cold, but Hope put her arm on his shoulder. 'Keep going,' she said; 'keep going.'

'Somebody's weaving a story because we can't see the real one, so we're getting all these other stories. We have a storyteller in our midst.'

'Saoirse told me plenty of stories. Skye's told me plenty of stories, too,' said Hope.

'They have. They have indeed, but they could also be observations. Genuine observations.'

Hope stood and looked out to the sea. Then she saw a vehicle coming up to the house. Another one behind it, almost a small crowd with it.

'You need to come inside, Perry,' said Hope. 'I can see the

press. They're coming for us. Come on, you know the drill. Inside.'

She grabbed Perry's shoulder but he kept standing there. 'Can't see it,' he said. 'Just can't see it.'

'You will,' said Hope. 'You will. Come on. Inside. Before they put pictures of us looking bemused at the sea.'

'It won't be me,' said Perry. 'The beautiful case, remember? No room for me in that.'

Chapter 18

It was getting dark when Hope got back to the Tides of Tranquillity, looking to catch Maddy before she went back to her rooms for the night. Not that that would have bothered Hope, for she'd get the woman up. As she walked in through the door, Hope saw that the reception was still being manned by Maddy, and she strode over to the woman.

'I'd like to talk to you,' said Hope. 'I suggest we let one of the constables stay here through the night. You can't cover reception all day and all night.'

'No. I can't,' said Maddy. 'I should sleep. I should . . .'

'You should,' said Hope. 'Let's go back to your quarters, once I've got a constable. Okay?'

'I thought Ruairidh might have come back,' said Maddy almost mournfully. 'Alasdair and Ruairidh sometimes did late-night fishing. It's one of the few things they talked to me about regarding the island, and they tried sometimes to get me to engage more. But I was always worried about bringing in the locals, because you change that perfect feeling, you know?'

'What do you mean?' asked Hope.

'They run cruise ship visits here, and it's a bit like that,' said Maddy, 'I know because I used to do that. I'm an experienced manager, really. That's my trade. When we used to get people on cruises to go and visit attractions on an island or in a particular area, you would bus them there. You would make sure that they got to see the shop. They would get to see what you wanted them to see. You didn't get the whole place.

'They were on holiday. They were there to have an experience. You didn't want any negativity. You wanted it all to be what their dreams said it would be. This place has to be that for our guests. If they don't get that, they don't come back. They don't keep using us. The money doesn't come in. It's a tough job,' said Maddy.

'I'm sure it is,' said Hope. 'Go to your quarters and I'll join you very shortly. Okay? I'm going to ask you some questions. I'll sort a constable for the desk here. Make sure nobody comes in without being attended to. They can always call you if the guests need you.'

Hope got hold of the local sergeant and placed a constable at the desk. She then took a moment to fortify herself, getting ready to talk to Maddy. As she did so, she felt one of those flutters again. Something from down below at her belly.

I haven't time for this, she thought. *I haven't time.* And then she thought, *of course I do. I have to have time. Because if it is right, it is right, I have to have time. Even if this is just a feeling, I will still have to have the time when it becomes real.*

After another moment, Hope walked the corridors until she found the accommodation that Maddy used. She knocked on the door and Maddy opened it still dressed in her blouse and tight skirt. However, behind her, a large drinks cabinet had been opened and Hope could see the large measure of gin in the glass.

'Do you want one?' asked Maddy. 'Just don't tell anybody

else. I won't tell them about you.'

'No,' said Hope, 'I can't.' A hand going to her belly. If she was, she certainly wouldn't be having any of that.

Maddy had clearly noticed the gesture, but she turned and almost flung herself down on the sofa, still holding her glass. Hope sat down in a small chair opposite.

'You have a lot to contend with here, don't you?' said Hope.

'It's not easy, like I say. You manage an experience for them. They have to perceive everything the way that you want them to. They have to enjoy it. They have to become part of it. This has to be a place that they own, not one that you own and that they somehow visit. When they go away, they will have to want to come back to say, "When I'm feeling like this, this is where I go." That's what I've been charged with.'

'Who charged you with that?' asked Hope.

'The Board,' said Maddy. 'The Board, that's what they do.'

'Who do you report to on the board?'

'Oh, they don't come out. That's the other thing; it's at a distance, normally just talk by email.'

'Is that not unusual. Surely it be better if you were face to face?'

'Honestly, it's easier by email. I was told at the interview that they wanted somebody to take the place and run with it, to manage it, to make it be. I was given free rein in bringing in whoever I wanted, and most of them I did. I was fortunate enough with Ozzy. He came to us because of that Sheik, and he was good. That's why I hired him. But the others, I did my research. I brought them in. Saoirse, Skye. The boys, Alasdair, God rest his soul, and Ruairidh.'

'How did you pick them?'

'Ability. Ability,' said Maddy, almost drifting back. 'When

I interviewed them, they had the ability. But they also had to have that capability to deliver an experience. Not many around here locally did. Alasdair bought in. Ruairidh did to a degree too, because he's just a pool attendant. It's not difficult, what he was doing, but he was good with the guests, wherever he's gone now.'

'And Skye, Saoirse, and Ozzy.'

'Skye and Saoirse. Well, Saoirse's got the red hair,' said Maddy, smiling. 'Some guests like that. She's got the accent, too. Forgive me, but without that mark on the cheek, you could work here, too.'

'I got that mark on my cheek saving somebody's life.'

'I don't care about that,' said Maddy. 'I'm sure you did wonders. I'm sure they're eternally grateful. I'm sure it gives you great pride, but I'm not running a place where what we feel is right. It's what the client feels. Saoirse. The Irish accent, the red hair, and that figure. Skye. The Welsh accent, those rolling black locks, the figure. Dark-haired Ozzy. Gorgeous man. Argentinian. That's almost Zorro-like, isn't it?'

She smiled to herself. 'And me!'

She really thinks this of herself, thought Hope.

Suddenly, Maddy sat up and spun her legs round. 'I have to be like this. It gets harder and harder, you know. I see Celeste and I feel for her. I see Celeste because they want you to be older and still as gorgeous as when you were young. They want you to be competent and still as lovely.'

Maddy stood up and marched back over to the drink cabinet, pouring herself another neat couple of shots of gin. The glass went quickly up to the lips. She turned back to Hope.

'Do they want the confidence from you? I bet they put you up, don't they, whenever they want to advertise the police force. What height are you? Six feet?'

'Yes,' said Hope.

'Six feet. Long red hair.'

'Glasgow accent, though. Maybe not sexy enough for you.'

'But you're not there to give an experience,' said Maddy. 'You're there to get cases solved.'

'Some people say you and Ozzy were lovers,' interrupted Hope.

'Yes,' said Maddy. 'I mean, why wouldn't I? A hell of a body. Younger man. I'm out here on my own. I have stresses and I need somebody to take care of me. I need somebody to help me through.'

'Was there a deeper want there?' asked Hope.

'It was just sex,' said Maddy, but she looked away at that point. The glass came up and she drank more. The glass went back down and became filled again.

'That's not what people have told me. Some people have . . .'

'Who the hell's told you what?' raged Maddy. 'Bastards can keep it to themselves.' She slammed the glass down. Hope wondered that it didn't break.

'Was it more though? Was it?'

Tears were falling from Maddy's eyes now. 'Yes,' She said. 'Okay. Yes, I loved him. He just . . . I don't know. He didn't do things the way you were meant to. Do you know that? That . . . rascal that you can't help but love. The others, if they didn't work by the book, if they didn't do my paperwork, if they didn't deliver the way they were meant to, they were out. Skye, Saoirse, they knew that. They wouldn't let standards fall.

'But Ozzy . . . Ozzy wasn't telling me everything. Ozzy wasn't producing the paperwork properly. Yet I loved him. I really did. I wanted him. I wanted that body. I wanted that man. I wanted . . .'

'You wanted what?'

'Don't you see? At my age, it would have validated me. I could pick him up. I could own him. He wanted to be with me. Even at my age. Even . . .'

Hope said nothing, but wondered at how insecure the woman really was. Out there before everyone, she was so professional. She was in charge; she was on top of things and yet, she wanted what? A man, a younger man to justify that she still looked good? Had she got caught up in the life of presentation? Had everything just been about looking the part? Had she convinced herself she actually had to be the part? After what she said a few moments ago, complaining how they always wanted you still to be that way, despite getting older.

'And the paperwork, it just what?' asked Hope.

'Didn't get done. We moved it aside. I like to know what people are doing. I like to know what clients are getting, because then I understand what it is they've received, what they're going to receive next time. You learn; you begin to get on top of that, but Ozzy, Ozzy was doing things and I didn't know what they were. I didn't understand it, and yet people were still coming back. I need to understand the experience, I need to be able to build that experience for next time. Do you get that?' asked Maddy, forcefully and with passion,

'I do,' said Hope. *Maddy was good at her job*, Hope thought, *and this weakness, this hunger for Ozzy, it was conflicting. It was making her not be in control of her job. She was falling apart because of her need to still be something. And yet, the way she ran the place, she was everything.*

'How did you get the job?' asked Hope.

'Headhunted by a company. Patterson Recruitment.'

Maddy turned and walked over to a filing cabinet. She pulled out a couple of drawers, shuffled through some papers, and placed a letter down in front of Hope.

'That's them. Patterson Recruitment.' Hope picked up her phone, tapped in the address and messaged it off to Ross, asking him to check it. 'They interviewed me in a hotel in Perth. There was a man. He laid out the way he wanted to run, wanted somebody to take charge of the spa. They didn't want any involvement so to speak; they wanted to be at a distance, to be able to communicate via email after that. The money would be delivered and the money was good,' said Maddy.

'The money was incredibly good, and I thought to myself, five years here, make your name. Maybe I could set up my own place; maybe I could actually be the part of the world I wanted to be. This place doesn't work for me, you know. I'd rather have an island out in the sun somewhere. I'm not an outdoor girl.' She laughed and turned back to fill up her glass again.

Meanwhile, Hope looked down at her phone for there was a message from Ross. *Quick scan, cannot find them, cannot find a listing for Patterson Recruitment anywhere.*

'Maddy,' said Hope, 'my colleague has just gone looking for Patterson Recruitment. As good as you are at setting an experience for people, DS Ross is an expert in hunting down information, especially from the web. He's done a very quick search and it's not complete, but he can't find hide nor hair of Patterson Recruitment. He's saying it's looking like they don't exist,'

'What?' said Maddy. 'Of course they exist. They pay me, you can go into my records, find the accounts, where we get paid.

Yes, I'm happy for you to do that. I was there. It was in a hotel.'

'We will check,' said Hope.

'Ozzy,' said Maddy suddenly. 'Somebody killed Ozzy. Ozzy being with me was showing me to be still on top of this. They're there somewhere. Patterson Recruitment exists. They came; they looked for me. They wanted the best; they got the best. I'm still the best,' said Maddy, almost shouting.

Hope stood up. 'I think you should get yourself off to bed. Been a long day,' said Hope. 'I'll talk to you tomorrow. We'll come for those bank statements and other details. We need to find out who's been paying you. Patterson Recruitment looks like a sham.'

Maddy stared almost incomprehensibly at Hope. But she turned back and poured herself yet more gin.

'That's the last one,' said Hope. 'Do not have more. I need you in a frame of mind tomorrow that I can speak to you. Okay?'

'Whatever you say, Inspector.' Maddy raised a glass to Hope. Hope meant to turn away, but her phone vibrated in her pocket. She pulled it out. It was a message from Perry.

Get back. They've found Jack. He's been in the sea.

Chapter 19

Hope McGrath pulled up at Stockinish on the east coast of Harris as the weather was taking a turn for the worst. Winds were picking up now, and she could see the waves crashing against the shore. Perry was standing just outside a police car, staring down at a lifeboat in the bay. His hair was being swept this way and that and at times it looked like he would fall over, so strong was the wind down on the coast. Hope thought she could hear a helicopter and had difficulty not slamming her door shut as she left the car.

'Perry,' she shouted. 'What's the deal?'

'We just picked him up,' he said. 'They're taking him up to Stornoway. He's definitely dead.'

He was shouting over the wind, and Hope was struggling to hear him. Her leather jacket was flapping open, sending a chill across her body. She tried to zip it shut but struggled in the wind.

'Get in the car,' shouted Perry at her. He went round to the driver's side of the police car, opened the door, climbed in, and then fought to get it shut. Hope took his advice and clambered into the passenger seat beside him.

'That's better,' said Perry. 'Can hear each other now.'

'Haven't you got your big coat with you?'

'Somewhere,' said Perry. 'You just get involved, don't you?'

'So, what's happened?'

'Well, the search party found him on the rocks, but they couldn't get at him. He'd been washed up against them, and with the wind freshening up and that, they weren't too sure about going down the rocks to get him. Eventually, he seemed to slip off back into the sea. The lifeboat picked him up, but the helicopter was already here, so they winched down, picked him up to take him off to Stornoway. It's a fair wee run back up for the lifeboat. Jona's waiting for him up there already.'

'So, he came from the sea, did he?'

'Can't say. That's what it looks like. Like he was thrown up onto the rocks, but let's see what Jona says.'

'I've just been speaking to Maddy Lyle. Strange tale, she tells.'

'In what way?' asked Perry.

'She basically runs the place. It's meant to have this board over the top. She's never seen them. She only communicates with them with email. There was one person who interviewed her. She quite likes it, because she just gets on and does what she does. But, it's almost like . . . well, there's a complete lack of involvement from the top down. Not sure they've even been here.'

'You found anything else out?'

'Yeah, she got the job from Patterson Recruitment. She's got the paperwork and everything to show it. Ross says Patterson Recruitment doesn't even exist.'

'So, who's looking after this, then? Where's the money going?'

'We need to work that out. I'm getting Ross onto that, but at the moment we don't know.'

Perry sat, looking thoughtful.

'What?' asked Hope.

'Hope, think about it,' said Perry. 'You've got no board over the top. So, it looks like this is a sham. It looks like somebody has set this up. But why? Why would you set up a health spa as a sham? To launder money? Better ways to do it than that. And it wouldn't be so obvious that there was no board. If you were a criminal gang, you would have a board. It'd be a sham. The purpose of it would be to drive money through, but that's not what's happening here. You're getting paid big bucks from guests coming in. There're movie stars. It's too obvious. It's too big. You will not launder money through here, so it must be to actually make the money.'

'And so what?' said Hope.

'If this is your moneymaker, think about it. Ozzy's dead. Ozzy's a star attraction. Oswaldo was someone that most of these stars went to. We've got our seaweed specialists, but there must be plenty practitioners able to wrap up people in seaweed. There must be several of them.'

'Of course; Saoirse said that. She indicated that she was one of many, but she only got the job because of her looks.'

'Exactly. And then you've got Skye Anderson, twenty-five-year-old, Welsh lass. Now, come on, Hope, look at her. She's got the skills, I'm not denying that, but she's going to be your yoga meditation instructor. Well, why not? She's got a cracking figure.'

'Maddy said as much, but she recruited them.'

'Exactly. She recruited them. Maddy was doing what she's meant to do.'

'She does appear to operate according to her job description, doesn't she,' said Hope. 'She also seems very driven.'

'That's it. She's very driven, and she understands the game. However, Oswaldo, she didn't hire Oswaldo.'

'Oswaldo came in,' said Hope. 'Oswaldo came in because a Sheik liked him. And then she took him on.'

'Exactly. And that's the problem. He's the one that died.'

'I'm not sure I'm following you,' said Hope.

'Connection's nearly there,' said Perry. 'Think about it. If you set this up, you bring in Maddy and she runs it genuinely. If you've got something else going on, you've got to bring somebody else in from the outside. But Maddy's got to think that she's brought them in. So how do you do that? Well, what's the one thing Maddy wants?'

'Clients to be happy.'

'Exactly. And, lo-and-behold, this sheik says he's happy. He's delighted with this guy. What does he do anyway? What treatments does he—'

'Nobody really seems to know,' said Hope. 'It was all quiet, very secretive. I'm not sure Maddy knows.'

'They all work on their own, don't they? They all work separate. All work without Maddy being there. I think Oswaldo was a ringer,' said Perry.

'A ringer?' queried Hope.

'Yes, a ringer. He's not there to give treatment. He's there to give something else. Something else is going on with him.'

'Like what?'

'Look who else is dead,' said Perry. 'You've got the local lad. Did he know something? Did he see something?'

'Well, that's always a possibility.'

'He was hired by Maddy,' said Perry. 'Once again, Maddy

hires him. She hired him. Why?'

'She hired him because he was efficient. Because he could do the job, and he looked good.'

'Exactly. The other lad, he's run off. He was hired by Maddy. I think he's hiding. I think he's on to something. He knows something. Oswaldo is a ringer,' said Perry. 'He's got that house he goes to. That could be the drop-off. It could be he knows somebody else here local. Maybe the women in that house are just fun and games, like they said they were. But someone bought them that house.'

'Do we move on it, then?'

'I wouldn't yet,' said Perry. 'We don't want them to run. If they run, people will understand we're on to them. Whoever's over the top of this will get clear?'

'But you said that somebody is in charge of this. You were trying to make the connections. Trying to make a point.'

Perry sighed. 'I was, wasn't I? Give me a moment.' He turned and looked out of the vehicle. 'The other person's got to be here,' he said. 'The other person, at the top, is here at the moment. Something's gone wrong with Oswaldo, and they've dealt with it, and this is the fallout.'

'Can't prove any of that, though, can we?'

'No, we can't,' said Perry, 'and I can't say for definite I'm right, but it looks that way. We need to get after this board, need to get Jack's body examined and find out what we can from it. We need to understand what the real purpose of this place is.'

'You're right, Perry. I'm going up to see Jona, get an initial idea of what's going on with Jack's death. Wrap up down here, okay? Keep the search going for Ruairidh. If you think he's hiding, then he could be in trouble. But he could also be the one who can help us find the killer. Assuming it's all the same killer.'

'It's the same killer,' said Perry.

'But look at the people here at the moment,' said Hope. 'Celeste. Just a movie star. An old movie star at that. We've got a kaput and frankly going-nuts Service man. He was in the Service. They're keeping tabs on him and would see illegal activity. They'd jump all over him, wouldn't they?'

'Well, you know the Service better than I do.'

'The other option is our young, timid girl,' said Hope. 'Maybe she's doing a good act. Maybe Daddy put her here. Maybe Daddy funded it. It was a sheik that came over that put Oswaldo in place.'

'But what's the point? If he's a sheik, he's got money,' said Perry.

'Well, keep thinking about it. Get wrapped up here and I'll go see Jona,' said Hope.

She zipped up her jacket, stepped out of the police car, and walked back to her own. She could feel the buffet from the wind. And saw the lifeboat, crashing back out through the waves of the loch, to head back up to Stornoway. She'd be there long before them. And the helicopter wouldn't be far off arriving by now. She wondered what Jona could tell her.

It took Hope just a little more than an hour to get up to Stornoway. By the time she arrived at the hospital and walked down to the morgue, Jona had already received the body. Hope waited outside while Jona continued to examine him, and only when she was finished did Hope talk to her.

'I've given him a brief examination,' said Jona. 'Come with me.'

'Why? Where are we going?'

'I've got a folder here with some photographs, and I need a

coffee.'

Jona led Hope along the ground floor to the small canteen that serviced the hospital. Grabbing a couple of coffees, Jona sat down at a corner table, Hope on the other side.

'Oh, that's needed,' she said, and Hope waited patiently while Jona took a few more sips. Then she opened up the folder, and Hope looked at the pictures showing a body in front of her.

'So, what happened to him?'

'There's a bump on his head. It's quite a nasty bump. Is it a blow? I'm not so sure. I think it's come from a rock or something.'

'So, like a what?'

'Like a fall from the cliffs,' said Jona. 'I did a little talking to the Coastguard station. I'm not sure he would have come out of that loch if he'd gone in fairly recently. I think he would have been buffeted back up to the rocks themselves. And that's where they found him. Again, whether he would have got out of that loch, I doubt it. In either case, it's perfectly feasible that he went in somewhere in that area. Without knowing the exact point, it's difficult to say where and exactly how he washed up. However, the wind has been picking up and the tide's coming in. So it makes sense that we didn't find him because he was in the water before. Searching through the water is difficult.'

'So what else are you telling me?' asked Hope.

'I think he fell, and I think he hit his head, but it wasn't enough to kill him. It may have knocked him out, or I think he drowned. I need to do a bit more of a thorough examination, but that's my running theory at this time. One other thing, though. I think he may have been an addict.'

'He was a boxer. What do you mean, you think he was an

addict? How would that work?'

'I don't know,' said Jona, 'in terms of his boxing. What I do know is that he had an awful lot of needle marks on him, and recent ones.'

'One's he's had since he's been here,' asked Hope.

'So in the last three weeks, maybe.'

'The first body was wrapped up in seaweed. There were small needle marks, weren't there? Or there could have been.'

'We certainly believe that Oswaldo had some sort of needle marks on him. And using seaweed would have been something that could have closed them over.'

'Is seaweed treatment normal at a spa?' said Hope suddenly.

'As far as I know, a lot of them offer it. Why?'

'Saoirse, she's specialising in it. Said she's just here for the money; she's here to do this. But if people were coming with needle marks and then having been wrapped up in seaweed, she'd notice it, wouldn't she?'

'I noticed this because I'm crawling over his skin. Whether she would have noticed it, not sure. She might have noticed a couple of the recent ones, but people get injections when they're at spas. She wouldn't have thought he was an addict since she wouldn't have seen a lot of the marks I have seen.'

'She still could be involved. That could be her role, to cover these things up. To be like the band-aid around the wounds.'

'I won't say you're wrong. What I will say is, he's an addict of some sort. He is taking injections, one after another. And that's in a form that I didn't find on Oswaldo. Oswaldo had some puncture marks, but not that many. Not consistent. Some things I've seen on Jack are quite old puncture marks. He would get injections with time, but I'm not convinced. I need to have a further look. The trouble with injections is, of course, over time they heal up.'

'I think we're getting close,' said Hope. 'Don't let this get out, okay? Keep it within the team. Don't let anyone in this hospital find out and leak it.'

'Of course I won't,' said Jona.

'Keep all our secrets together. I've got someone missing and I think he may be a material witness to the murder. To the first one, anyway. I need to shake this down,' said Hope. 'There's a board that sits over the spa that doesn't exist. I need a reason for the spa to exist. Something more than just making money, because you don't have a false board, because you simply want to make money. It's got to be more than about being a health spa. It might be about making money in the wrong way.'

'Well, that body in there says somebody could be an abuser of some sort, taking drugs for whatever reason. I'll get back in, see what we can find out, see what's in his system.'

'Be as quick as you can with it,' said Hope.

She drank her coffee, stood up, and went to leave Jona, but was called back.

'By the way,' said Jona, 'you're looking well at the moment, despite everything that's going on. Your hair's almost got a sheen to it.'

That's just ridiculous, thought Hope. *Things don't work that quickly.*

'It's just got tossed in the wind,' said Hope, as she walked out of the canteen. She felt the excitement that the case was coming together, but more than that. She also felt something again. Was she imagining it? She didn't have time to find out.

Chapter 20

Hope watched as Macleod stepped down from the village hall stage, away from the press before him. He was shaking his head, confident he was out of sight.

'I thought you handled it well,' said Hope.

'Oh, for the days when I could send you up there,' said Macleod.

'You still can.'

'No, I can't. This is your case. I'm here to help. But it's bizarre. Some of those people there—they're not journalists.'

'They are journalists. Or paparazzi. Or—'

'Did you ever get as many flash guns going off in your face?'

'I didn't intend to handle all these sexy cases, or at least do the press conference on them,' said Hope, teasing Macleod.

'I could have lamped that one in the front. How did I think Celeste would be affected by all this? Would it be detrimental to her part in the film? What sort of question is that? I'm a detective chief inspector. I'm not the critic for the movie house.'

Hope burst out laughing. But then she turned and walked, leading Macleod to a kitchen at the back of the hall.

'I'm sorry it's instant, but . . . it's something.'

'Just give it to me,' said Macleod.

Hope had already made the coffees, expecting Macleod to have been off the stage at least ten minutes earlier. But they were still warm enough, and he gratefully took it to his lips. When he put it back down, she stood looking at him for a moment.

'What?' said Macleod.

Hope caught herself on. She'd been thinking about if something was inside her now. Had a little one been formed? Macleod was here. Part of her was going to tell him. She couldn't tell him yet. She hadn't told John.

Hope didn't want to tell John, not until she knew she was . . . confident. Until she knew it was real, what she was feeling. But why would she want to tell Macleod? As if he would have any idea whether she was making sense. He didn't have kids. Never mind not being a woman.

'It's nothing. I think we're getting close in the case, though,' said Hope, changing the subject. 'I've got Ross looking into the board again. We've got to get into that. Check the money. Check where everything's going. I don't want to rattle cages at the moment, in case somebody does a flyer.'

'No,' sighed Macleod. 'But we do have a young man that needs to be found.'

'I don't think he's on the island,' said Hope. 'Been missing a while.' She was afraid for young Morrison. He had disappeared at the same time as Jack.

'I don't think he's involved in the killings,' said Macleod. 'Perry said he talked to the locals. He seems like a typical lad. I wonder if he's seen something. That's the thing about Ruairidh and Alasdair. They would have good reason to be going about the island. They might have seen something, not living inside the centre. Everybody else, if you were a killer,' said Macleod, 'you could almost predict where they'd be and when. But staying away from the general populace, staying away and . . .'

'You think somebody saw Alasdair?'

'No,' said Macleod. 'I don't. I don't think they saw him as such. I think they were keeping an eye. The young lad's different. The young lad's there doing the pool. Alasdair, however, would know everything. Alasdair was Maddy's right hand. She always wants him on the desk; that's what you keep telling me. I think Alasdair died because, well, because he knows something. I'm not sure what Morrison knows. He may just be scared. Or he may have seen something.'

'Well,' said Hope, 'he has been absent for a few days now. Like I said, he's not here. I'm wondering did he run for the ferry? Did he jump on a boat over the Minch? We may need to put his likeness out a bit further afield. We may—'

Hope stopped suddenly. Her phone had gone off, and in these last couple of days, every time that phone had gone off, it spelt some sort of development in the case. She picked it up and looked to see who was calling. It was Perry.

'What's up, Perry?' asked Hope.

'We've got him. We've bloody well got him. Found him inside a radio shack, hiding up. Kid's scared as anything.'

'Where is it? Where have you got him?'

'Rodel. There's an aerial just around the corner from Rodel. Well, it's quite up, actually. But there's a little hut there. That's where all the equipment for the aerial is. He was inside that.'

'Seriously? Didn't anybody check it?'

'Somebody had been in it. Looking at the radio. But they

were going back over old ground, checked it again. Realised that somebody was in there. He was so scared he hadn't even come out to use the toilet.'

'Blimey,' said Hope. 'Where have you got him?'

'Taking him back to our place. We haven't let many people know where he is. He's with Ross at the moment. I've just popped outside to call you.'

'Keep him there. Get another couple of constables up around our building,' said Hope. 'I'm on the way with the big boss.'

Hope closed the call. Macleod looked at her. 'I wish you would stop calling me that, especially in my presence.'

'We got him,' said Hope. 'Perry found Ruairidh. Apparently, he's terrified. But he's back at our digs.'

'Best we go there then,' said Macleod. 'Do a quick interview. After that, get him up to Stornoway. Get him out of this area, somewhere safe with a couple of constables.'

'Come on then,' said Hope. The pair of them jumped into Hope's car and drove the short distance to their digs, where Perry met them outside.

'He's in the living room. I've settled him down somewhat with a coffee. Ross is with him. Who do you want with you?' he asked Hope.

'You say Ross is inside?'

'Yes,' said Perry.

'Well, you stay out here, then. Just keep an eye out. I take it there are another couple of constables kicking about.'

'A couple out the back. You can get access that way. I thought it best to keep a lookout everywhere.'

'I'll stay at the front with you,' said Macleod to Perry.

'You sure you don't want to join us inside?' said Hope.

'Your case. I don't want to . . . you know.'

Hope nodded and entered the living room of their digs. Over in the corner was Morrison. He was only a young lad, with tussled hair that was dark, and an attempt at a moustache that Hope thought could have been better. With sticking-out ears, he wasn't that attractive, Hope thought, different to the rest. She had assumed he would look better than he did, but then again, he had been sitting in a shack for the last couple of days, or whatever it was they kept the radio gear in. She got a whiff of urine from him as well.

'I asked if he wanted to go for a shower,' said Ross, 'but Ruairidh said he was fine. He's worried about where we go next.'

'I'm going to have a quick word with you, Ruairidh,' said Hope. 'When that's done, one of our team will take you up to Stornoway. We'll get you a hotel up there for the meantime, well away from here. We'll not tell anyone else where it is, and we'll put some officers with you.'

Ruairidh nodded, but he said nothing.

'I need to know what you are frightened about.'

'I'm not frightened,' said Ruairidh. 'Bloody terrified.'

'Why?' asked Hope.

'I saw it. Oswaldo. I didn't know. I didn't understand what was happening. But I saw it.'

'You saw what, exactly?' asked Hope.

'Man or woman in a coat. Long, dark coat. Hard to see because it was raining.'

'Where were you?' asked Hope.

'I do night fishing sometimes. All the time. Ask anyone. I like that. To night fish. I was sitting on a rock, line out, and saw this figure, up in Loch Ghreosabhagh. Don't normally see that many people about, certainly not stumbling over to the edge of the loch. They dropped something. I thought they were just, like, dumping rubbish, you know? Well, I couldn't see who it was. I was going to tell somebody about the rubbish, because it's not good. You don't throw waste into the sea. You don't throw any plastics in there. It kills the fish.' Ruairidh was shaking now.

'Go on,' said Hope. 'It's okay. You're safe now, but go on.'

'Well, then they said that Ozzy was . . . missing. I mean, just missing, but then, then he turns up dead. You know? And I put two and two together. But I didn't know they'd done it. Never thought they'd dumped Ozzy in there. It didn't hit the sea. The rubbish didn't make the sea. I think they meant to. But there was a car came along after they'd thrown him. They were, I think, going to go down, but they didn't. They had to go. I'm not sure the car came past, though. I think it turned off early. But they left. They didn't come back. And then I went into work, and next day, discovered Ozzy was dead, and well . . . I had to run.'

'Did you know anything about Jack?' asked Hope.

'No. What's up with Jack?'

'Jack went missing too.'

'I didn't know that Jack was missing,' said Ruairidh. 'But Alasdair, well, he was different, after Ozzy, what had happened with him? He wouldn't tell me, Alasdair; he wouldn't say. I should have talked to him, I should have said what I'd seen, but I was worried. Thought I'd keep my head down.

'I don't really fit in here. Maddy, she's not that keen on me. I mean, look at the rest of them. Yeah. You have Ozzy. He was good looking. All the ladies liked Ozzy. Alasdair was always good looking when we grew up. Everybody talked about handsome Alasdair. I was just, well, I'm okay, I guess.

But the women, Skye and Saoirse, I couldn't believe it when I got to work there, and I saw them. Even Maddy. Oh, she's a bitch, but she's a good-looking bitch.'

Hope could see that from a young teenage lad's point of view, it must have been a dream place to work. Hormones going ten to the dozen. But what about when things went wrong? No wonder he was scared, especially if he didn't feel he fitted in.

'You know about Alasdair?'

'I'd heard something. Jack, I can understand. He's very hot-headed. I mean, he threw a punch at your man, didn't he? But Alasdair wasn't like that. Alasdair was thorough and did his job. Alasdair wouldn't just leave. And then I heard rumours the next morning that something had happened on Rodel. And I legged. But I didn't know where to go. You get on the bus but buses have CCTV and things these days. I get on the ferry. Everybody knows who I am down here. I can't go anywhere here without people knowing who I am. So I went into the radio hut.'

'You could have come to us,' said Hope.

'You don't understand. The people that work in that place. The people who are there. They have big money. They get what they want. If I didn't do the pool right, or I didn't leave something right, they would tell Maddy and Maddy would jump all over me. But if they'd done something wrong, Maddy would cover it. I'm sure of it. Maddy wants everything to be right for them. Sometimes I wonder how far that went.'

'I believe Maddy employed you, didn't she?'

'Yes. She was struggling, you know. The thing is that for the front desk, she found Alasdair. But she needed somebody who understood about pools and how to keep them clean and do the paperwork. But she didn't want someone from far away, because that would be very expensive. You'd have to pay somebody a fortune to come and do a pool here.

'I had done a bit of work one summer when I was away. So, I knew what I was doing. She took me on. People didn't really get to see me, you know. Saoirse, Skye, Oswaldo, Alasdair, Maddy—they're interacting with the guests all the time. Not so with me. I did a lot of the lifting and loading and the pool, of course. I wasn't with the clients. Guess that's why she was okay with having somebody ugly like me.'

The boy isn't ugly, Hope thought. *He's a decent enough looking lad. Very stereotypical. Must have been hard in a place like this, though. Maddy probably looked down on him. Possibly some of the rest, too.*

'When you ran, what was the trigger to do it?'

'I knew Alasdair knew something,' said Ruairidh. 'But I saw the long, dark coat. The one that was worn by the person dumping the rubbish. It was hanging in the spa. I became paranoid. I couldn't keep a lid on it. That's when I ran for it, that's what tipped it, the radio hut was close. I didn't want to come out after that, I didn't want to come away from it,'

'And what was your plan?' asked Hope. 'To stay there forever?'

'Everyone was looking for me in that place; I was sure of it. When I got to the radio shack, I could hear the common communications you need to put out a search for me. You're never sure if they're going to come to you. I mean, I was expendable. Alasdair was clearly expendable, so I stayed hidden, although there was a big search on for me.

'One day someone came in and I was just curled up behind the radio set. They didn't look thoroughly, but this last time they looked the whole way. It's probably because they, well . .

. one of the corners I used as my toilet. I knew I should have fled from there, but I'd heard you'd found another body, but they didn't tell you who it was over the radio.'

'So you could hear the communications inside the hut?' asked Hope.

'That's normal,' said Ross.

'Yes, but I had to turn the volume up,' said Ruairidh.

The man was shaking now and Hope gave Ross a nod, and the pair of them left the room together. Once outside, she turned to Ross.

'We need to get him up the road. I don't think he's got anything to do with this. But we need to go in and get the coat, and then see who it belongs to.'

'I'll get on that right away,' said Ross. 'I'll get Perry to go up with him.'

'Have we done a search? A thorough search of the premises?' said Hope. 'We did look, didn't we? Everywhere?'

'There's no coat. We didn't find a big coat. We weren't looking for one,' said Ross, 'but we didn't find one.'

'Look again,' said Hope. 'And get after those board members.'

Macleod stepped in from outside. 'How did that go?' he asked.

'Very well. Ross here is going to look for our board members, and for the money associated with it. Perry's going to take Ruairidh up to Stornoway and sort him out up there. He saw who did it, but he didn't recognise who they were. Just in a large coat. However, I want you to find that coat. Make it act like you're the bigwig coming in. Like I haven't done my job well enough.'

Macleod almost laughed. 'So they don't know we're on to them. They don't know what we know.'

'Exactly,' said Hope. 'You think you can pull that off?'

'This is the big boss you're talking to,' said Macleod, grinning as he turned on his heel and walked out the door.

Chapter 21

'I don't see why you have to do this. The place has been searched,' said Maddy.

She was standing with her hand on her hip, staring at Macleod, as if this was going to influence him somehow. Macleod was looking at the team of officers around him, sweeping through the place.

'What are you looking for, exactly?' she asked.

'I'm getting a proper search done this time,' said Macleod. 'Sometimes you need a ranking officer to do things properly.'

He was enjoying this, ready to ham it up, as the overzealous senior officer. But underneath, he was looking here, there, and everywhere. Maddy, for all that she showed confidence, had initially come forward, almost flirting with him—as if feeling that her mere presence and looks would influence him somehow. Maybe Hope didn't get that from her, not being of the opposite sex. But Macleod definitely got that impression.

And when that hadn't worked, she'd got angry. He wondered if that was because she felt rejected. The place was weird. His Jane was lovely. He adored her. Physically, mentally, her whole being was what he liked. But this woman didn't seem to even think about the other parts of herself, other than what he could see.

'Why are they coming through my room again?' It was Celeste, marching out of her quarters and coming directly for Maddy. 'There's a police officer come in and asked to search my room again. Why are they searching my room? This is preposterous. This is—'

'That's the man who's ordered them there,' said Maddy, pointing at Macleod.

Celeste marched over and Macleod thought it was a little early in the day for an evening gown. However, he was also aware that it was a rather revealing evening gown. Nothing unusual if she'd been going to win an Oscar, but for kicking around a health spa?

'Is there something I can do? Something I can assist you with?' asked Macleod.

'And you are?'

'I am Detective Chief Inspector Macleod.'

'Where's the red-headed woman? McGrath, or whatever you called her.'

'I'm Detective Inspector McGrath's boss. I'm the big boss,' said Macleod, relishing every word he said.

Celeste put a hand up on his shoulder and leaned into him.

'I understand you have a job to do, Detective Chief Inspector, but you've nothing to fear from me. There's nothing in my room.'

'Then you won't have a problem with me searching.'

'What are you looking for?' she asked.

'Looking to get a search done correctly.'

'Well, I hope you won't be revealing any of this to the press.'

'Why would I do that?' asked Macleod.

'I had that incident two years ago. The next thing, the

contents of my underwear drawer somehow got revealed in the press. Yes, I'm sure one of the police officers got paid for that.'

'Where was this?' asked Macleod.

'Oh, it was back Stateside. I think, well, I'm not sure but one of them had a bit of a fetish for me.'

'Well, that won't be a problem here,' said Macleod.

He walked off and Celeste nearly fell over. He heard the words of disgust behind him but was suddenly met by someone else reaching out from a door. Macleod stepped back and realised it was Edward Pembrook.

'On the hunt. On the hunt. We'll find them. We'll find them wherever they are. You know that?' He looked up at Macleod. 'Who are you?'

'Detective Chief Inspector Macleod. You can calm down, sir. It's all in hand.'

'They're everywhere. They're everywhere. You know that?'

'This is why I didn't want the search,' said Maddy. 'You've set his paranoia off. This is what we're helping him with.'

'Need to do a better job,' said Macleod. 'If this sets him off, I mean, what's going to happen if something proper kicks off?'

'Two deaths isn't something proper?' blurted Maddy.

'Dead! They're coming for me! It was me they were coming for! You understand that, don't you? Macleod, you hear me? They were coming for me!'

'So I've been advised, sir,' said Macleod. He strode off, and this time saw a pair of eyes staring at him from behind another door. It was Zara El-Amin and Macleod didn't quite know what to think of her. If she was behind this, she was playing a fantastic disguise. Maybe she was innocent, but could there be a sheik controlling this, some Middle Eastern power, using the place? Seemed unlikely. And the girl said nothing.

The local sergeant walked up to Macleod.

'Excuse me, Detective Chief Inspector. A word.' Macleod stepped to one side with the man. 'We found nothing, Seoras. Absolutely nothing there.'

'Fair enough,' said Macleod. 'I didn't think we would. You can round the team back up. I think I've caused enough havoc for today.' He wondered if Hope was getting any closer with her lines of inquiry.

* * *

Hope was sitting beside the phone, waiting to see if anyone would come back with any answers. She had sent out some of the team on the mainland looking for the board members. Ross, on his laptop, was sitting across from her. He had been working hard for several hours. Macleod would be back soon, and she hoped he would come up with an answer. If he came with the coat, at least that would be something, but no coat was probably more likely. The phone rang in front of her.

'This is Hope.'

'Susan here. I've traced down some of those addresses for board members. They're completely false. The people living there have no idea who we're talking about.'

'Have they ever received any mail, though?' asked Hope.

'Sent it back as there was no one of that name living at their address.'

'How's your leg doing, anyway?' asked Hope.

'This is the first day really, out and about. They're thrilled with it. I mean, it's going to take a bit of getting used to. The crutches did too, but I'd sort of got on top of them. This is, well, this is different again. To go from using your arms to suddenly putting weight back on the leg, except there's no feeling at the bottom. It's different, Hope. It really is.'

'Well, thanks for looking into that for me.'

'Well, it wasn't far from where I was, was it?' said Susan. 'I'm here, available if you need any more.'

'You just sort out getting yourself properly mobile on that leg. And then we'll see. Okay?'

Hope put the phone down. She wished there might have been some sort of contact through the board members, but there was nothing.

'No luck?' said Ross.

'Nothing from Susan. Still waiting to hear from the other two.'

'Was Clarissa all right with you, nabbing them?'

'Nothing much on. I don't know; she didn't quite put it like that. But yes, she was okay with it.'

'You two seem to get on a lot better these days,' said Ross. And then he almost wound his neck back in, as if he'd said something he shouldn't have.

'It's difficult when you've got two sergeants,' said Hope to him. 'Now we've got two detective inspectors and we're doing completely different jobs. We're very different people. Learn to live and work together. You'll need to learn to live with Perry.'

'He is different,' said Ross. 'I can see the way you use him.'

'What way's that?' asked Hope?

'Well, he makes lots of connections, doesn't he? Not like I do. I find things, bits and pieces of evidence. I trawl. He doesn't, comes at it like a mental exercise. He sees connections and then has to prove them.'

'And that's why you'll make a good team together,' said Hope.

She thought back to when Perry came onto the team. It was Macleod that had placed him there. And she'd been told by Macleod that Perry would replace Macleod for her. Well, Perry didn't replace everything she received from Macleod. The team was always changing.

She sat for a moment again, and she had that funny feeling. It was annoying her now as she was working. And yet, inside there was almost a joy. A promise looking to spill out. She would enjoy having this case done because then she'd find out. She'd look to see if something had occurred. Now was not the time to check.

The phone rang again, and Hope picked it up.

'It's Sabine. I've gone round all those addresses you gave me. I'm still waiting to hear from Emmett.'

'Did you come up with anything?'

'No,' said Sabine. 'These board members don't exist. At least that's the impression I'm getting. Not a word about them.'

'I'd have thought somebody would have looked them up beforehand. I'd have thought—'

'But why? There would just have to be one,' said Sabine. 'If they all had the mail sent to them, but one was real, then whoever was running the deception would still get the information.'

'There was a chairperson,' said Hope. 'That was James Uxbridge.'

'James Uxbridge is being looked at by Emmett. Maybe he'll come back with something. But I've got nothing for you. They don't exist. The addresses have completely different people there. It's not the address of the people you're saying should be there.'

'Susan Cunningham told me the same,' said Hope. 'Thanks, Sabine. Sorry to take you off your work.'

'Not much happening at the moment. This gave me a bit of a diversion. Otherwise, I was going to have to look at some paperwork Clarissa was sending down. She's trying to get me to teach Emmett the arts.'

Hope wanted to say something, but she thought better of it. 'Thanks again.' She put the phone down. She looked across at Ross and shook her head.

'I'm finding nothing,' said Ross. 'All the online presence is a fraud. Nothing real. The deeper you go into this, the more and more you find out there's nothing there. And trying to trace where the money's going is a nightmare. I've got the first account it goes into. But the money shifts after that. I can't find it. I think it's heading towards Switzerland. And a Swiss bank account is just a number. I can't get in there.'

Hope stood up, went over to the window, and stretched. Pretty soon, she was going to have to come across something. Something was going to have to break. Everyone was being kept in the one place. Whoever was doing this at some point had to get out.

They couldn't just leave, could they? Couldn't just wait it out. They'd have to close everything and make a run for it. They couldn't start the 'treatment' again. Jona had phoned back and said there was definitely something in the system of Jack Harrison. But she couldn't identify it and it had gone off to be tested.

The phone rang again. This time, it was Emmett. Hope hadn't met Emmett, but he had seemed bright enough on the phone.

'Hello, Detective Inspector. This is Emmett Grump.'

'It's always Hope. What have you got for me, Emmett?'

'Two of the addresses made little sense. The people living there had lived there for several years. They got an occasional bit of mail and sent it back to the Royal Mail, saying it was wrong. I don't have any of the correspondence. It's been destroyed by now. However, one of the other addresses you gave me turned up something.'

'Which one?' asked Hope.

'James Uxbridge.'

'You find him?'

'No, not as such,' said Emmett. 'It was quite weird, because you go to the address and there's a flat. And inside, there are four flats. And you have A to D inside on the doors. Flat A to D all have letter boxes, but there's also a flat E, except there isn't. Flat E is James Uxbridge's. But there's not an actual flat. They haven't seen much mail in it, and I spoke to the people in the other flats. Apparently, every now and again, this man would turn up.'

'A man?'

'Yes. When I asked them what he looked like, they all gave completely unique descriptions. It was like different people turned up every time. Except,' said Emmett, 'when I questioned them about his height and his physique, it was the same. The clothes changed, the face changed, his age changed. But never the height and never the physique.'

'You're thinking it's the same person?'

'That's what it would seem like,' said Emmett. 'I haven't got CCTV here. Or at least, I've only got recent CCTV. So, the CCTV that would have filmed him is gone. Deleted to make new storage. So all I've got to go on is the descriptions given by those who live in the other flats. Sorry, I can't give you any more than that.

'Like I say, it's just a box. I talked to the postie, and he doesn't know who put it there. He's always just delivered with no questions. The flat owners believe that it's the owner's letterbox. But when I went to the Tenants Association who run the building and all the other flats around here, well, they knew nothing about it. It's just a box that's appeared. And it's like nobody clocked it there.'

'And we've got no idea who put it in there. No way of getting around that.'

'It's not the most dynamic of flats, you know. It's one of these places where the landlord only pops in every year or two. He doesn't do much, very absent. It's got an agency who runs and looks after it. Nobody clocked this flat E. Everybody thought it was somewhere else, or it was a box for the owner. And the owner hasn't been here to clock it.'

'Thank you, Emmett. I think you've confirmed something for us.'

'Any time,' he said. 'Just make sure you tell Clarissa I was useful.'

Hope nearly burst out laughing. She put the phone down and Ross looked up at her.

'Anything?'

'One letterbox. One person, coming in different disguises to pick up the mail from that letterbox. Nobody knows him. Nobody knows anything about him. Same physique. Same height. That Emmett guy's good, though. He thinks a bit differently.'

'I'm thinking that those are the sort of people you like in your team. Getting worried about my position,' said Ross.

Hope glanced over and then saw the grin on his face.

Whoever was co-ordinating this was here. Hope was sure of it. There was a man picking up the mail. But the men here were who? Sir Edward Pembroke. The man was mad. And just because a man picked up the mail didn't mean it was Sir Edward. There could be a small team behind this.

One thing Hope knew now, though, was that she would solve the case right here. She couldn't let anybody disappear. Whoever was running this was very good, and trying to nail them to the mast was going to be difficult.

Chapter 22

The day was progressing, and Hope saw the wind and the rain continue to batter the landscape. She gave a sigh, then turned back to the desk behind her.

'That's what it's like here,' said Macleod. 'I grew up with it. You get these times of the year with just constant winds, rain. It sweeps through, then there's sunshine, but a cold wind. You hope for a north wind, or an easterly. They're more settled. The south winds, especially coming into winter, they come strong, and they come wet.'

'It's no wonder you're such a moody bunch,' said Hope.

Macleod raised his eyebrows at her. 'We're thoughtful, deep thinkers,' said Macleod.

Hope gave a smirk, but turned back with a pensive face. Something had to break in the case. Somebody was going to run for it, and she was going to outstay them until they did it. They could let people go now, if they wanted, but that would just let whoever was doing this go away.

The scam was up. Whatever was going on here was over. They couldn't operate under the conditions they were now being put through. A police investigation into several murders. It would be relentless, even over a longer period. But if she let them go now, if she said everyone could go home, well then, they could run, with whatever money they'd already taken. Maybe they'd set up somewhere else.

Perry had been sent down to the Tides of Tranquillity, mainly to keep an eye on everyone. Uniform were there, but Hope always felt happier having one of her detectives about. And besides, Perry might notice something. His mind was chewing over what was going on. It was making connections. Being in the environment would help him.

She'd learned to give him a bit of free rein. She was turning into a good leader. At least, that's what she reckoned. Using the skills of each of her team. She knew her own skills. Dogged. Determined. Go through things procedurally. Keep on it. Don't give up. And also shut out the other voices. Trust her gut.

'Well, if nobody else is making coffee, I'm going to,' said Macleod.

'Alan's busy,' said Hope. 'I'll take mine white, thanks.'

Macleod nodded and headed for the kitchen. The thing about having Macleod around was he was great to talk to, but he wasn't so good at covering off the more menial tasks. He hadn't come down here to replace someone. He was down covering off the press and giving an overview. So, it was like having your boss there the whole time.

He wasn't as demanding as that. But he would still look for the updates every now and again. To see where she was at, what she was thinking. In truth, she was having trouble thinking at times. She was having to force herself. Because the other thing on her mind kept coming back again and again.

And no wonder. They'd been praying for this for a while. But she didn't know. It could all be in her head. And she didn't want to find out right now. And besides, what did she say? 'Oh, by the way, I'm popping up the store now. I need to get a little medical thing.' It wouldn't really wash, would it?

Hope's phone rang, and she picked it up. On seeing Perry's face on the screen, she asked, 'Any developments?'

Perry was huffing and puffing. 'Damn right there is. There's been a note left by Celeste. She says she's going to end it all.'

'What? Celeste? Why?'

'Don't ask me, but it's been pinned out by the front of the premises.'

'Pinned out by the front?'

'That's right,' said Perry. 'And the press has got it.'

'How did it get pinned out at the front with nobody seeing her?'

'Oh, they saw her,' said Perry. 'They saw her. They've got it. Photos of her doing it, and then she disappears. By the time they got over and read it, she was gone.'

'Oh, heck,' said Hope. 'You need to find her.'

'I'm kind of on that,' said Perry. 'Pulling teams together. I'm going to start an initial search from where we are.'

'This we don't need,' said Hope.

'Don't worry,' said Perry. 'She's not dead.'

'Why? Why do you say that?'

'Trust me,' said Perry. 'She's not dead. But if we don't get to her, she will be.'

'I'll be over shortly,' said Hope, putting the phone down. She paused for a moment, wondering exactly what Perry meant. Then she shouted, 'Seoras! Celeste's trying to top herself. We need to go.'

Macleod came in with a fresh pot of coffee and grimaced at having to put it down and leave it.

'What do you mean, she's trying to kill herself?'

'She left a note. All the press have got it.'

'No,' said Macleod. 'No!'

'Come on. Ross, you stay here. See if you can dig any more up.'

Hope grabbed her jacket and then tore off out into the wind and rain for the car. Macleod followed shortly. He had his jacket wrapped up around him. Hope thought he would be better at handling the cold, but he was wrapped up like a precious package. If he was brought up here, surely he could handle this.

Hope drove out of Leverburgh and round past Rodel, up towards the Tides of Tranquillity. As she did so, she could see Perry standing at the roadside, pointing. Behind him were lots of press who were running amok now. When everything was contained inside the centre, they could control the press— what was given to them, who they saw. Now they were on the loose, filming live as the police responded to a suicide note. They would love it. The drama, the sheer excitement of it all.

'I think Perry's found something,' said Macleod. 'That was quick.'

'He told me not to be worried. Told me she wouldn't be dead,' said Hope.

'Ah,' said Macleod, clearly realising something.

'Don't do that,' said Hope. 'You and Perry. I mean, what's "ah" mean?'

'Means he's right,' said Macleod.

'Don't do that,' said Hope, pulling the car up to the roadside. She jumped out, slamming the door behind her. Macleod got out ahead of her.

'Perry, what's happening?' asked Hope.

He pulled close, realising there was a camera team not ten feet from him. In the wind, he had to speak firmly, but he kept as quiet as he could.

'That boat has drifted off from the quayside. I'm going to get down, get on a boat and go to it. I think she's on it.'

'Why do you think she's on it?'

'Because she's not going to kill herself.'

'What is it, then? Cry for help?' said Hope.

'No, it's an actress making the best of an unpleasant situation. She is getting whatever the centre is supplying,' said Perry. 'But of course, she's realising that we're on top of it now. So, she needs to be a victim. She needs to be someone who can sell her story. What better way than to act like you're going to kill yourself? Think of the drama of this. If this case blows her movie part, she'll still be able to write a book. She'll be everybody's news for forty-eight hours. She can spin the tragedy of it all.'

'Well, let's get out there to her.'

'I was going to see if we can get a boatman,' said Perry.

'It's a boat. It's got an engine on the back,' said Hope. 'It won't be a problem.'

She started walking down towards the quay, far below her. She realised Perry was in tow, but Macleod was well beyond him. Hope stopped for a moment to allow Macleod to catch up.

'Can you deal with the press?' said Hope. 'I'll take Perry with me.' There was almost a drop in Macleod's face. 'I know, Seoras, but I need to interview this woman. You need to get these vultures out of here. I don't want this to be the story of the day.'

'It's too late for that,' said Macleod. 'They're on it, and they'll stay on it. If you're going to talk to her, I'd do it out in the boat.'

'Grand,' said Hope. She went to turn, but Macleod shouted after. 'Do you know how to use a boat?'

'I'm not just a pretty face,' said Hope. She stuck her tongue out at him.

Hope found a small tender tied up and watched a rather unbalanced Perry get on board. She started the engine and then steered the tender out into the loch, where the other boat was now adrift. It was much bigger, a fishing boat, and clearly Celeste wasn't a complete idiot for she'd untied it and got inside.

Hope took one of her ropes and tied it to the side of the other boat, and she jumped on board before helping Perry. The fishing boat, small as it was, had a little area beneath the wheelhouse where you could sit, make coffee, or even wrap up in a bunk if you wanted to. Celeste was there. She was wearing a jacket over a rather enticing looking top and tight leggings.

'Evening dress unavailable?' asked Hope.

'Don't stop me,' said Celeste.

'Go on then,' said Hope. 'You're not going to do anything. This is for that lot out there. The press has got full pictures of this. But you're not going out there until you give me what I want in here.'

Celeste's face collapsed. 'I'm the victim here,' she said.

'I don't think so. Not in my book. Before we go out there, you're going to tell me why you come here.'

'I come here to get better. I came here to do a part in a film.'

'No, you didn't,' said Hope. 'You came here for something else.'

'No, I came to get ready. I came here to get ready for the film,' said Celeste.

'She did,' said Perry suddenly, beside Hope. Hope could have killed him.

'What do you mean by that?' asked Hope.

'She came to get ready for the film. Our boxer came to get ready again, both of them needing to get back into condition. That's why she came.'

'Exactly,' said Celeste, 'for the rest, for the—'

'For the drugs,' said Perry firmly. He stared at Celeste. She leaned towards him, almost flaunting at him, but Perry was completely unmoved.

'You're right,' said Hope. 'She came for the drugs. Boxer, needing to get back on top. Film star, ageing, but needing to recover her strength to get back to the type of film star she was.'

'Hey,' said Celeste. 'You won't find a better body than this at my age.'

'But it is your age,' said Hope. 'You can't keep going like you used to. You can't cut the mustard, so to speak.'

'So that means she's come for the drugs, just like Jack,' said Perry. 'Oswaldo must have been the one who handed them out.'

'Okay,' said Celeste. 'I'll tell you, but you can't tell the press. We'll make a deal.'

'Not okay,' said Hope. 'We'll parade you in front of the press, if you don't tell me now. We'll go to the station and do this formally. We'll make sure you're not the victim. If you want to salvage what's left of your miserable career, you do it now, by telling me everything. It'll look like we've talked you down after your great suicide attempt.'

Celeste looked calculating. She was trying to read Hope's mind, or at least that's what Hope thought. She stared over at Perry, and then she turned to Hope.

'Okay, Ozzy got them. Ozzy was the one giving them to us, okay? Jack was on them. I'm on them.'

'And what do they do? What drug is it?' asked Hope.

'I don't know what they call it. It's a wonder drug, a new drug. It helps, pumps you up, and they can't find it. That's why Jack wanted it. He was struggling. Some of his injuries, the battering he took—he didn't get back to full form. He told me this. He knew what I was here for. And I knew what he was here for.'

'So did Ozzy contact you?'

'No,' said Celeste. 'It's done by the centre. There was a Barbara. Barbara Mayer. She was the one.'

'Who's Barbara Mayer?' blurted Hope. And then something clicked with her. She looked at Perry.

'She's on the list, isn't she?'

'One of the people who doesn't exist,' said Perry.

'She damn well exists,' said Celeste. 'Here!'

She pulled out her mobile phone. After tapping it for a bit, she held it up to them. There was a woman in the picture. It was grainy and the light dim. Perry stared at it.

'You know what?' said Perry. 'In the right light, that could be Susan. From that house.'

'What? The one that Ross—'

'Yes,' said Perry. 'The one that Ross went to. I saw the pair of them briefly when I was doing my rounds. Had her pointed out to me. That could be her. I mean, there's a slight change in the hair. A bit of darkening of the skin here and there. Bit of make-up.'

'That's Barbara Mayer. She organised it all,' said Celeste. 'Nothing would be mentioned when we were here. Nothing was mentioned. Maddy said nothing. I just came in, and then when I was with Oswaldo, I got my injections.'

'Maddy doesn't know at all,' said Hope. 'Maddy is the perfect person. She's got a perfect screen. She's running what she thinks it's a legitimate business, giving her clients what they want.'

'I was told not to speak to anyone about what we did here,' said Celeste. 'It would just happen. I know they did other treatments, but these, these were special. And we always had a seaweed wrap afterwards.'

'So' said Perry. 'They're running the drugs. It could be Susan who's linked to it.'

'So if it's not Jack, and it's not our Celeste here,' said Hope, 'who's behind it? Who's the kingpin?'

Chapter 23

Hope brought the fishing boat back to the quayside where a rather relieved fisherman was standing. He was, however, brushed out of the way by the mass pack of reporters. Hope manoeuvred the boat directly alongside and then was assisted in tying it up by some local fishermen.

She could see Celeste attending to her hair. As she stepped off the boat, Celeste seemed to pick the correct angle so her hair blew out behind her. Her jacket was lying open. The remaining clothing pressed tight against her body as she faced the wind. She was definitely an actress. Born for it.

'They were able to talk you down. How did it feel, Celeste? How was it?'

'Did you think of your fans while you were trying it?' asked a voice.

'Give us another shot there, Celeste. Turn sideways.'

As Hope clambered off the boat, she was disgusted at the almost feeding frenzy that was going on. Macleod stepped in front of Celeste, between her and the press contingent.

'Get out of the way!' said somebody.

Macleod turned on his heel, looking at him.

'Get out of the way!' came the cry from several reporters.

'One! It's "get out of the way, Detective Chief Inspector Macleod." Two, I do not have to get out of the way. You, however, do.'

Hope could see more officers coming down towards the quayside and knew that Macleod had timed this correctly.

'You will all take a step back,' said Macleod, 'and we will depart with Miss Beaumont. Anybody getting in the way will have conversations with me up in Stornoway. I, however, do not have the time for a conversation today, so it'll be tomorrow at the earliest. But don't worry, we'll make sure there's accommodation for you at the station.' He stood staring at the press.

'You're having a laugh, aren't you, Inspector?' said a voice.

Macleod swung his stare along them. Hope was impressed. They couldn't be sure. They really couldn't be sure. He had that annoyed look on his face, but Hope thought it was put on. Underneath, Seoras would be happy. Actually, he would be keener to find out what Hope now knew than happy.

Macleod turned to Celeste Beaumont. 'Do your coat up,' he said. 'You'll catch a chill.'

It was like an instruction to a little child. While at first, she hesitated, Macleod's stare made sure that she did her coat up, now properly dressed as Hope was sure Macleod would have put it. Macleod accompanied Celeste up the quayside and towards a car at the top. Hope clambered after him, accompanied by a wheezing Perry.

'I don't like boats,' said Perry quietly behind her. Hope was aware of a camera now on her face. She heard the click and turned her back towards the photographer.

'Can you just turn the other way, please?' said a voice.

'No,' said Hope. She knew why, she knew what was behind it. The scar was on the other side. He didn't like the scar. Some of them thought it ruined her. To Hope, that was an almost unforgivable statement. She turned and pointed at Perry behind her.

'That's your actual hero there. You should be getting him on your front covers.'

Perry nearly burst out laughing as a couple of them took a photograph of him. The idea Perry would ever be on the front cover. He wasn't that sort of officer. He was anything but glamorous though he was quite a fine detective.

Hope joined Macleod in the front of the car, while Perry clambered into the rear seat with Celeste. They drove her back to the Tides of Tranquillity, escorting her into a room, before they convened in one of the small offices that had been put aside for the police.

'You get anything then?' said Macleod. 'Other than stopping her from stealing the limelight.'

'She's here for strength-enhancing drugs. New ones. Ones that don't show up yet. Ones that she's obviously not able to get hold of. I'm going to phone Jona and tell her.'

'Who's supplying them, though?' asked Macleod.

'Oswaldo did,' said Perry. 'But she was initially approached by a Barbara Mayor. She showed a photo on the phone. It's Susan from the house. I'm sure of it.'

'It's Susan from the house? Those two girls couldn't have run it. They're not up to this,' said Macleod. 'Somebody else is at the core.'

'I agree,' said Perry.

'More to the point,' said Hope, 'I agree. That leaves us two people. Whoever's running this show is here at the moment, dealing with the problems. Maybe Oswaldo went over the top. Maybe he was going to blow the deal. So, they've taken him out. Alasdair must have known about it as well. He's dead. Ruairidh saw them. So we've got to keep him under wraps. And as for Jack—'

'Jack may have been losing it,' said Perry.

'What do you mean?' asked Hope.

'Boxers. Yeah?' said Perry. 'Boxers don't just punch somebody like me. That's insane. I'm an officer. You get into a lot of trouble. He's not at a fight and he's not primed. And yet he was wound up as anything. He was losing it. I wonder if this drug isn't as neatly tied up as it should be.'

'You think there're side effects?' asked Macleod.

'It's supposition, I know,' said Perry. 'But maybe Jack was going to become a problem. He then disappeared, didn't he?'

'And whoever did that is here,' said Hope. 'I don't think it's Maddy. She's too out of the loop. She's the perfect cover woman. Unwitting. Daft. Saoirse? Well, Maddy brought her in. Skye? Again, Maddy brought her in. Here for Maddy's vision of the place.

'Maddy wouldn't need to set somebody up on the outside that Ozzy went to, if Ozzy was hers. But Ozzy wasn't. Ozzy came in from the outside. From a sheik. Somebody played him into position. And that's either a sheik or a man. The father, of Zara El-Amin, if that's who she is. If she's not some sort of assassin, taking out and dealing with the situation. If not, it's our spy gone paranoid.'

'It's going to be hard to deal with the sheik side of it, isn't it?' said Perry. 'Out of the way. And if this is what she's here to do, she's not going to say.'

'We can deal with our spy, though,' said Macleod. 'We have

links. Time to find much more out about him. We need to—'

'You can ring Anna. Anna Hunt,' said Hope. 'Push her for more information. See if—'

Macleod folded his arms. 'No,' said Macleod. 'She doesn't get to speak to who she wants to get to speak to. This is your case. You ring her.'

'She prefers you to me,' said Hope. 'She doesn't like me, I don't think. Doesn't think I'll go with her cover-up ideas. Keep everything quiet. You moonlighted over in Italy. You can keep secrets when you want. She thinks I'm too by the book.'

'Good,' said Macleod. 'Put her under pressure.'

'What?' said Hope. 'This is the Service. It's the head of the Service we're talking about.'

'She wants cooperation. She can co-operate with the police. You're heading this investigation. You talk to her.'

Hope stared at him.

'Perry,' said Macleod, 'give us a minute.' Perry huffed and left the room while Macleod stood and looked at Hope. 'You can't let who someone is determine what you do. You need to go at her.'

'You'll get more information out of her,' said Hope.

'Why?' asked Macleod. 'You need to get that information from her. It's your job. It's—'

'But you would get it a lot easier.'

'Really? I went off behind her back. She knows you as someone who does it for the job. This is a case; there's an issue. She needs to know that this is a real issue. This is not somebody like me trying to cover, or help a colleague. This is about the national interest. Hope, this is where you come into your own. Don't hold back,' said Macleod, before Hope could answer.

He left the room before she could respond. Hope shook her head, picked her phone out of her pocket, and dialled a number. A voice on the other end asked who it was. On giving her name, Hope was asked to wait before the voice said they would call back. It was a minute later when a number rang on her phone, one that she didn't recognise.

'This is Anna Hunt. What's the matter?'

'I need to talk to you about Edward Pembroke.'

'I told you—he's paranoid.'

'I need to know why he's paranoid. There's a situation here,' said Hope. 'Someone at the Tides of Tranquillity has been dealing strength-enhancing drugs.'

'What type of enhancer?' asked Anna.

Hope didn't know, but the door of the office was knocked, and Jona stepped inside.

'Hold on a minute,' said Hope. She put her hand over the phone, but thought she heard Anna complain.

'You need to know,' said Jona. 'Jack was on some sort of enhancer. I don't know what sort of enhancer it is. Nobody knows what sort of enhancer it is. This has got forensics going bananas. This is major.'

'Come here a minute,' said Hope to Jona. 'I've got Anna Hunt. On the phone. She's the head of the Service. You need to tell her what you know about this strength enhancer.'

Jona nodded and Hope stepped away while the diminutive Asian woman gave two minutes of information to Anna Hunt. Jona then turned and handed the phone back to Hope.

'Are there any other suspects?' asked Anna.

'Zara El Amin. But only if she's not who she says she is.'

'Zara El Amin is the daughter of a sheik. She is exactly who she says she is,' said Anna.

'How do you know that so quickly?'

'We keep tabs on our people. She's in the same place as Edward is. She's who she says she is.'

'Then Edward is running drugs. I've ruled out the others here.'

'Bugger,' said Anna. Hope was astounded, there was a collapsing of the voice as she said it that took Hope's breath away,

'Bugger?' said Hope. 'Tell me, do any of these names make any sense to you?' Hope rhymed off James Uxbridge and a host of other names from the board of the Tides of Tranquillity. There was silence at the other end for a moment.

'That's the cover of his team,' said Anna. 'He lost his team. That's why he's paranoid. He lost his team overseas.'

'How many of them?'

'Two women. A man. I'm not giving you the names,' said Anna.

'Young women? Like under twenty-five?' asked Hope.

'Yes. Why?'

'Hang on,' said Hope. She turned to Jona. 'Jona, get Perry in here now.'

Perry came in promptly, and Hope told him to get the photograph of Barbara from Celeste's phone. It took a few minutes of messing about between the phones to get the images transferred, but Hope sent the image off to Anna Hunt.

'That's Alice Moorcroft. She's a former operative on Edward's team. She died overseas. He lost her out there.'

'I don't think he lost his team at all,' said Hope.

'Tell me all that's going on,' said Anna.

Hope relayed the case so far, including Celeste's attempt at a fake suicide.

'So, it's come out. He'll see it's come out. If Celeste is doing that, and you've brought her back, and Celeste is one of the clients,' said Anna, 'he'll cut and run.'

'Well, we've got the young lad who saw him, but didn't recognise him, safely secured. Celeste is with us. Maddy, the centre manager, is with us, but I don't think she knows anything, anyway. He kept it clear of her.'

'But the team? The team has been set up. Alice has been made by you, by me. You said that you'd visited them, both of them.'

'Yes,' said Hope.

'Then they are loose ends,' said Anna.

'Well, they'll run, won't they?' said Hope. 'They'll just run with him.'

'They were dead to us,' said Anna. 'Dead to you, dead to the world, who they actually are. Do they know,' said Anna, 'that this has all been coming to a head? How much information will they know?'

'What are you suggesting?' asked Hope.

'You don't live in my world,' said Anna. 'If I'd set this up, if that was my ploy, with the drugs and with the money, and I'd used them, this would have been a long-term thing for them. They moved to the island. Somebody bought them a house. They weren't high in the service. Operatives in name, but brought in from the outside by Pembroke to make a team. It's not uncommon to do so. But clearly, they were ready to make more money than we give in the Service.'

'And?'

'You've made yourself a team. It doesn't work. You get rid of the team,' said Anna.

'What?' blurted Hope.

'You clear out, you get rid of the team. They can finger him. If we were in a foreign country, and people could do that to us, we would take them out. This is what he'll do, he'll get out, he'll get away, because he won't want anything that can be connected to him, in case we find him.'

Hope dropped the phone down from her ear and shouted, 'Perry, get in the car!'

Chapter 24

We need to get to the girls' house,' said Hope, turning and running for the car. Perry sprinted, and they jumped in. As Perry raced the car along the narrow roads scattering the press behind him, wondering why a police car was racing so quickly, Hope called for Macleod.

'Get to the house,' she said. 'Claire and Susan's. We need to get there. They're in trouble.'

Hope relayed what she'd found out as Perry continued his manic drive around the bends of the harsh coast. As he raced into Leverburgh, then turned up towards the house, they could see that Ross was on the road standing beside the other hire car.

'There's nobody in the house,' he said, standing at the front door.

'Is the door open?'

'Yes, it is,' said Ross.

Macleod appeared, but was shaking his head. 'Doors open round here mean nothing.'

'Has he got to them already, though?' asked Hope. 'Come on, we need to see, we need to find out if they've gone somewhere or if he's got to them. Ross, go ask the neighbours. Perry, come

206

search the house with me.'

'I've had a scan through already,' said Ross.

'Exactly,' said Hope. 'Fresh eyes. You go do the neighbours.'

Hope never felt comfortable about commanding Macleod to do anything and was glad when he stepped inside the house with her. Quickly, they raced through it. Ross was right, nobody was here. Beds had been disturbed, so they must have been there last night.

'He may have called them,' said Macleod. 'Called them to meet somewhere. After all, he knows we know about this place. He could be watching it.'

'He doesn't know we know about its true purpose, though,' said Hope.

'But think about it,' said Perry. 'If he was the boss, he'd never meet them here. Oswaldo came here. These two are part of his old crew, so he's not going to meet them like this. He won't be seen at this house. He's going to meet them somewhere else, somewhere close, in the—'

'But not in Leverburgh,' said Hope. 'It's so small, there'd be spotted by someone.'

She glanced over at Seoras, who was nodding. 'He'd have to keep it separate from here, but close enough, so they could still meet.'

'He could go up to Stornoway or somewhere like that,' said Perry.

'No,' said Macleod, 'if he's come over as himself, as Sir Edward, he's not going to go to Stornoway. That would be noted. If he went out for a walk, if he went out for a good constitutional, people would not bat an eyelid, would they? And he's going to walk away from the villages. None of the spa people went to the villages.'

'Only Saoirse. She played her badminton, but that was it,' said Hope.

'So, he needs to meet somewhere around here,' said Macleod.

Perry went through to the kitchen and was looking at the notice board. There was a grocery list on it. Hope looked over his shoulder as well.

'Not much here, is there? There are a few contact numbers. But they're basic things. Local.'

'The shop, the local church,' said Hope.

'They never struck me as the religious sort,' said Perry. 'Why's that there?'

Macleod came over, and peered over past Perry. 'What's that code for,' said Macleod. 'I'd recognise a code from round here. That's not a Lewis number, or a Harris one for that matter.'

'Hang on a minute,' said Perry. He picked up his mobile and dialled. There was no answer on the other end. The number was unattainable.

'So, what do you think,' said Perry, 'is that like some sort of old number, the contact now being closed down.'

Hope was looking at it, staring at the digits.

'Couldn't be a grid reference, could it?' said Hope.

Perry raced out to the car, pulling a map from the glove box, and raced back into the kitchen, throwing it down on the table.

'Call me the numbers,' he said.

As Hope did so, Perry tried the references across the map, jumping into different boxes on the OS map. There was nothing at the front to say which box he should be in, but he tried different ones. After ten minutes, he stood looking.

'I don't think it's that. I can't find anything. Nothing relating to a church, nothing relating to anything else. It's just a—'

'Hang on,' said Hope. 'Look at the front end. You've got eight digits. And then another four.'

'There's eleven numbers on the phone number,' said Macleod. 'So, what are you saying?'

'First one,' said Hope. 'If you add two to it, you get a two. If you add three to the next one, you get a—'

'Zero,' said Macleod.

'Yes, four to the next one. You go round and get back to a two, five to the next one, you go round and get back to a four, twenty, twenty, four.'

'That's a year,' said Perry. 'And the next one, if you then add a five and a six, and then you go for the seven and the eight and you keep turning them round, you get—'

'Today's date,' said Macleod.

'And about five minutes from now,' said Perry. 'That's a meeting time. It's a meeting time. That's a meeting time. At the church!'

'What church,' said Hope. 'How would they meet in a church here? Can't be a church, can it?'

'There are a couple of churches. There's also the free Presbyterian church home of rest,' said Perry.

'But how would he have contacts in there?' asked Macleod. 'This isn't making sense.'

'Doesn't have to make sense,' said Hope. 'Into the car.'

Macleod directed them down to the free church in Leverburgh. As they got to the building, they found it to be locked up. They spun round to the free Presbyterian church rest home. It, of course, was open, the residents being looked after. Macleod had been there before visiting a former colleague. There was nobody unusual here, and the staff knew the women from the house that kept themselves to themselves. They hadn't been through.

'Church' said Hope. 'What church?'

Macleod's face lit up in the car. 'The temple. It's not a church; it's the temple.'

'What temple?' asked Hope.

'Head out through Northden. If you keep going there, out beyond the beach, and keep following the road, you get out to the temple. It sits out on a spit of land.'

'It would be perfect.'

'Where's this temple?' said Perry,

'You have to go across grass, and then the beach to get to it. It's on a tiny spit of land; it's old,' said Macleod. 'We're out of tourist season—highly unlikely anyone will be there. If there is, you can just wait. Easy place to meet up; if you stand inside, nobody will see you. But you will see people approaching for miles. You could even approach it by boat from one side, get yourself onto the beach, and walk out to it. Nobody will suspect anything. You're just a tourist. It's perfect.'

'How do you know about it?' asked Hope.

'I'm from here,'

'You're from Lewis,' said Hope. 'That's the best part of an hour up the road.'

'It's a touch longer, actually,' said Macleod. 'But where do you think we came? On day trips, time away? Been down to Leverburgh plenty. And places like this don't change.'

Perry was ignoring them both, the car hurtling along. Macleod suddenly pointed out from the back of the car.

'Left here. That's down through Northden. Through the village.' Perry raced on. He almost stopped when he saw a sign for Temple Harris.

'No, no,' shouted Macleod. 'That's a coffee shop. Keep going.'

Perry continued racing along. The road was little more than

a track but Macleod was still urging him on. The wind and the rain were incessant, though, the wipers of the car racing back and forward. 'Switch off your lights,' said Macleod.

Perry did so, and they were now not really on a path at all, more racing across the grass. There was a track, heading out and closer, and Perry could see the temple in the distance.

'The car's not going to get all the way there.'

'We could get up to the beach in front of it,' said Macleod. 'Go, go!' The car bounded off a pothole, jammed off to the left, and conked out.

Macleod had the back door open, and was running hard. Hope took off after him, catching him easily. Racing past him, he shouted, 'That's it over there! Over there, do you see?'

Hope could see it easily. But the ground wasn't easy to run on. She left Macleod in her wake and could hear a puffing Perry behind him. She continued towards the temple.

It was a ruin. As Hope approached, one thing struck her. Where would Edward go? He had obviously walked out here. Hope couldn't see a boat. If he was in that temple, he was fleeing. She would walk into a confrontation. That's if the women were there.

As she approached, Hope felt the rain driving into her face, and she squinted her eyes. She was sodden now. Thankfully, she had her leather jacket on but it wasn't zipped up and she could feel her jeans sticking to her legs. A shiver ran through her body, and she wasn't sure if it was the cold, or knowing she was about to walk in to face a killer.

Yes, he was an older man. But he'd taken out a boxer. He'd taken out Alasdair. Both were young, fit men. The man was an operative. She'd have to be careful. Very careful. Hope ran up to the wall of the temple, crouching down behind it, listening.

'It won't take long,' said a voice. 'Pity. You both did well. If Oswaldo hadn't screwed it up, we all would have been rich. As it is, I'll move on. Start again somewhere. There'll be demand for it, of course, especially with the notoriety that'll be coming from these recent events. What we have done here. Killing everyone. All for the money. All for this new wonder drug. And they'll want to get their hands on it. I'll have it. It'll be available,' said a voice.

Hope edged around the wall, turned a corner, and saw an entrance. Sir Edward was inside. Behind her, she heard the thudding plods of Perry. He was breathing heavily, Macleod now behind him. The voices inside stopped suddenly.

Hope stole quickly along the wall, getting to the entrance, hoping to block off any retreat. She saw something emerging, something coming out from the gap. Instinctively, she stood up and grabbed whoever was coming through. Except it wasn't. She found it was a jacket on the end of a stick, and then some someone stepped closer and threw a punch deep into her belly.

She was grabbed inside, winded from the punch, but stumbled, tumbling over, falling down onto the hard ground. Hope went to get up. Something kicked her across the face. She rolled back, slamming into the wall behind her. There were a couple of more punches hit hard down into her stomach, possibly just below. She couldn't punch back, but the animal instinct in her reached out. She grabbed a collar. She hung on to it. Hands went down to her throat, throttling her. Edward's hands pressing hard into her throat, choking her, and then she heard a cry.

Perry had never been described as a fit man; he had a bit of bulk to him, and Hope did see that entire bulk being driven for all he was worth, towards Sir Edward, currently throttling

Hope. Perry crashed into Sir Edward, shoulder dipped down as the man turned to face him.

The two of them clattered into the stone wall behind, and landed on top of Hope. Sir Edward's head made a sickening thud on the stone and he was left lying on top of Hope, Perry on top of him again after that. She was in pain in her stomach; she was gasping for breath. And as she looked across to the entrance of the temple, she could see Macleod stumbling through. He raced over, his hands going down towards Sir Edward.

'Ambulance,' gasped Hope.

'Not before we get cuffs on him,' said Macleod. He rolled Edward over, took a pair of handcuffs out of his pockets, and slapped them on the former spy. Hope, only now, was able to look around the temple, and up against the corner of a wall, she could see Claire and Susan, neither of whom were looking back. They were open-eyed, but staring straight ahead, not a movement from them.

'Seoras, ambulance, those two.'

Macleod was on his phone already as he raced over to the women. Hope staggered to her feet, and as she got to the women, she could see injections. Marks on the side of their neck, several. Hope reeled, crashing to the floor.

Macleod could be heard talking to police control, asking for medical help, suggesting a helicopter, suggesting further police presence, and cordoning off the area. When he'd done that, he turned to Hope.

'Are you okay?' he said.

Hope was holding her midriff and below. 'I'm okay,' she said. But there was a sickening feeling in her. Several of those punches had been down, down where she'd been feeling.

She was feeling strange. There was a sudden shock running through her. Could she still feel that feeling? Was that feeling still there? Macleod was looking at her with a worried face.

'Are you all right?' he said. 'Really, are you all right?'

She turned and sat down beside the women, almost like a copy of them. Macleod was looking down, staring at the wall opposite.

'I don't know,' said Hope.

Macleod's hands were down, checking for cuts. 'You're not bleeding. I don't find anything,' he said.

'Not like that,' said Hope. 'Not like that.'

'Like what then?' said Macleod.

Perry knelt beside her and took her hand. 'It'll be okay,' he said. 'You'll see. It'll be okay.'

'What'll be okay?' said Macleod.

As Hope looked at Perry, she could see eyes looking back that said, 'I know. It'll be okay.'

Chapter 25

Hope sat up in the hospital bed. She had wanted to stay at the temple, but Macleod had insisted. The helicopter had arrived and had taken away Susan and Claire in what were still almost catatonic states. Ambulances and Coastguard helped Hope off to an ambulance that made its way slowly up through Harris and through Lewis to the Western Isles Hospital. The paramedics had checked her over, and while they were concerned, they weren't seeing her as an emergency.

Macleod had been bemused by Hope's reaction. A few times, she had clutched her stomach and shed a few tears before fighting them back. He was also bemused by Perry, who had helped her, almost treating Hope gingerly, in a fashion neither she nor he had seen before.

But now she was sitting and resting, for they'd come and taken bloods. She'd spent several hours, her hand running in under the hospital gown, roaming across her belly and just down below it. She wasn't feeling those feelings she'd felt before. Her belly was tender, too. The punch from Sir Edward had been packed. He certainly knew how to hit for an older man. She couldn't imagine Seoras ever being able to hit like that.

In a way, they'd got lucky. He'd assumed she was the problem. And Perry, being Perry, had just launched himself into the situation.

A face suddenly appeared at the end of the ward. Hope was in a general ward, as far as she understood, without curtains pulled around her. There were a few other women in some of the other beds. But she hadn't got round to saying anything to them.

But Hope was tired. The last lot of days had been full on. She hadn't had that much sleep, and now she was just sore. A few times she'd went to drift off to get that sleep that she needed. But her mind was racing. Why didn't she have that feeling? Why wasn't there anything coming from within her body? Where were those strange feelings?

She looked up at the figure in the doorway of the ward. He had a hat on and a long coat, and now strode down to her bed at the far end.

'I didn't have time to get any grapes,' he said.

He put his hat on the end of the bed, took off his coat and laid it over a chair that was close by. Then he stood beside her. 'You okay?' he said. 'I haven't seen that sort of reaction before. Not from you. He must have hit you harder than I thought. I mean, he's close to my age. I wouldn't have thought—'

'He was an operative with the Service,' said Hope. 'I guess they know how to hit. He totally winded me, took it completely out of me. And then when he was throttling me, I, well, I've been grabbed a few times, but these people, they know, they know how to do it properly.'

Macleod nodded. His hand reached down and held hers. 'But you're feeling okay,' he said.

'Sorry to miss the party,' she said. 'I would have been there, like to have been there for the clear-up, to, well, come through it all. I take it you've interviewed him.'

'That's been interesting,' he said. 'We got to the interview room in Stornoway station, just started running the recording and in walks a rather sombre figure,' said Macleod. 'She wasn't happy.'

'Who?'

'Anna Hunt. She said she needed to have a word with me. Well, I said it's a police investigation, and we needed to interview him. She came to a compromise with me. She sat in on the interview with me and Perry. It was done without recording. I'm not sure how this is going to be handled. It's a bit of an embarrassment for her. And for them.

'He was running drugs, a new type of serum. Very experimental. Very hard to get hold of. But Sir Edward, in his time, had come to be a supplier. He set up the Tides of Tranquillity and was basically using it to serve people of need who had serious money. Very hard to detect, and Anna doesn't want too many more people knowing about it. He ran it while being under the watch of the Service. She said to me they'd been distracted of late; things had changed. Kirsten told me that as well, in Italy. The Service has a few internal problems. It appears the eye went off the ball with this one.'

'But what happened with Oswaldo then?'

'Thing is, Hope, as per usual, people get greedy. Oswaldo knew how to administer the drug properly. He had done it in other places. So, after setting up the Tides of Tranquillity and using Maddy to hire the staff, Edward sent over a sheik as a client. He was actually the sheik that came. Oswaldo did treatment with him, obviously not of the same type, and

Maddy felt she should take him on. Very clever play by Edward.'

'Absolutely,' said Hope. 'And he set up the girls, Claire and Susan, to feed the drugs in to Oswaldo.'

'Basically. And he came every now and again himself to check what was going on. As somebody who needed counselling, no one questioned why he was there.'

'So he could have his sessions with Oswaldo, find out what was happening, make his deals in his private consultation,' said Hope.

'We went back and talked to Maddy as well,' said Macleod. 'She was totally unaware, a woman doing a terrific job in a lot of ways, completely oblivious this was happening. She's a bit messed up by it. But Edward said Saoirse and Skye were completely ignorant of what he was doing. Same with Alasdair for a good while, and he was totally unaware that Ruairidh had seen him.

'Alasdair, however, had become aware in more recent times. Oswaldo had thought that something was up, but Alasdair didn't know who to go to. Then when Oswaldo died, Alasdair clearly contacted us. He was worried as well. Alasdair, Edward thought, worried about the standing of the people involved. That's why he didn't come to us openly. Sir Edward saw Alasdair talking to you and saw him deliver the letter. So he kept a closer eye on him and followed him. He killed him before you got there, and moved him away from the church to make it look like it was more random.'

'What happened then with the boxer? Jack Harrison?'

'One of the problems with the serum is if you take too much of it and too quickly, you can become angry, unstable. Not everybody suffers that side reaction, but he did. Edward was worried that Jack was going to lose it and blow the cover of everything. So, having already having to take out Alasdair and Oswaldo, he silenced him. After that, he needed to see if he could weave a story to keep the lucrative drug dealing going. When he couldn't, and things got closer to home, he cut and run.'

'That's what Anna Hunt said he would do. And take out everybody around him. I mean, they were his team that he was trying to kill. How are they, anyway?'

'Whatever he'd put in them wasn't good. They haven't come round yet. The hospital is hopeful they will. But they may get flown out down to Glasgow for something a bit more specialist. It doesn't matter from an investigation point of view,' said Macleod. 'Obviously, we want them to recover, but if they do, we'll be having wars with Anna Hunt to get them into a criminal trial.'

'There is still the idea of his box though, where the mail went when he did the applications. He was picking mail up from somewhere.'

'No, he wasn't. A member of his team was picking up. All three that Anna Hunt thought were dead, weren't dead. The women were here. His other colleague, the male one, was picking up the mail and organising certain aspects away from here. I asked Anna about him and all she said was, "He's been dealt with."'

'That quick?' said Hope.

'It's Anna Hunt,' said Macleod. 'Who knows? Maybe it means he will be dealt with and they're on it. Maybe he has. I don't know. There's going to be some discussions at a higher level between Anna and our people. And we're going to have to work out a story for the public that covers this. But the Tides of Tranquillity may be closed.'

'They could always give it to Maddy. She can run it properly.'

'We'll see,' said Macleod.

Hope looked beyond him and saw a doctor entering the ward. He came down towards Hope. 'Miss McGrath, I need to have a word with you. Is this gentleman family?' asked the doctor, pointing towards Macleod.

'No, this is my boss.'

'If you don't mind, sir,' said the doctor.

'Oh, of course,' said Macleod. 'Will she be fit for further conversation?'

'I don't know,' said the doctor. 'If you'd just give me five minutes with my patient. Please wait out in the corridor.'

Macleod nodded, picked up his hat, put on his head, grabbed his coat, gave Hope a smile, and walked out to the corridor. The doctor pulled the curtains around the bed, and then saw Hope's worried face.

'What is it?' asked Hope.

'You received several hits to the abdomen. You've got quite severe bruising down there. During our blood tests, we picked something up. Do you know that you're pregnant?'

Hope stared at him. 'Yes,' she said. 'I think I do. I haven't done any tests, but . . . this last while, something, something has felt different. But I can't feel that now.'

'I want to take you down for a scan,' said the doctor. 'You've obviously received quite a bit of damage. We're not worried about you from an internal point of view. Physically, you're okay. I don't think there's been any damage in that sense. But at such an early stage of pregnancy, we'll want to check everything's okay. Is your partner or the father about?' asked the doctor.

'John's back in Inverness. It would take him a while to get here.'

'I'd rather go straight down for the ultrasound,' said the doctor, 'just to check if anything's wrong. Is there anyone you would like with you?' said the doctor.

'The man that was in here, he's Detective Chief Inspector Macleod. Seoras is his first name. Ask him to come down with me.'

'Of course,' said the doctor. He turned and pulled back the curtains and marched out to the corridor. Some nurses came in and began to help Hope into a wheelchair to take her down for the scan. Once they'd done that, Macleod stepped into the ward. He looked down at her. 'Congratulations,' he said.

'They need to check everything's all right,' said Hope. 'I'm scared, Seoras, terrified. I have wanted this and I'm terrified I'm going to lose it straight away.'

'Can I push?' Macleod said to the porters who had arrived.

'Of course,' said the man.

Macleod got behind the wheelchair, kicked away the brake and put his hand over and took Hope's hand in his. 'We'll see,' he said.

He pushed her out of the ward and down the corridor before halting. He turned back to the porter, who was now exiting the ward. 'Can you tell me where I'm going?' he said. Hope laughed.

It was twenty minutes later that Hope was lying beside the ultrasound operator. The specialist was dressed in scrubs, looking at an image. Hope could feel the cold of the gel across her belly, and the sore press of the device into her bruised skin. The operator had asked her to say when it was too much, but Hope had told her to do what she needed to do. Hope's left hand was in Macleod's.

The operator didn't say much as she worked away, telling Hope that she would start off by doing her work, finding out what she needed to know. Hope's heart was beating fast. Despite the cold of the jelly on her belly, she could feel a sweat on her forehead. The operator took the scanner off and turned to look at Hope.

'I'm delighted to say I think everything's fine,' said the woman.

Hope burst into tears and felt Macleod squeeze her hand.

'I'm going to turn the screen, and you can have a look.'

The woman put the scanner back on Hope's belly. The screen, now turned round, Hope watched the smallest of images. Something was there. So tiny, small parts not defined yet. After a few moments, Hope just lay back, tears streaming down her face. She glanced over at Macleod.

'Well done, Mum,' he said.

'I guess I've given you about five or six months to find a new DI.'

'Only a temporary one,' said Macleod.

Hope's face suddenly contorted before she smiled back at him. 'I haven't even thought about that,' she said. 'Yes, I think I'm co—'

'I was thinking,' said Macleod, 'maybe we don't need a replacement during that time. Maybe somebody from up above could step down.'

Hope laughed, and she felt the operator wipe the jelly off her belly. 'I'll have you cleaned up and sorted here in no time,' said the woman.

'And then I need a phone,' said Hope. 'I need to tell John. He needs to . . . he needs to know.'

She glanced across at the image still on the screen. *We've done it,* she thought. *We've actually done it.* She'd read about it in a book. The woman who'd been writing talked about the time that she found out she was pregnant. She'd called it the greatest upheaval ever in her life. *Oh well,* thought Hope with a smile, *here goes!*

Read on to discover the Patrick Smythe series!

Patrick Smythe is a former Northern Irish policeman who

after suffering an amputation after a bomb blast, takes to the sea between the west coast of Scotland and his homeland to ply his trade as a private investigator. Join Paddy as he tries to work to his own ethics while knowing how to bend the rules he once enforced. Working from his beloved motorboat 'Craigantlet', Paddy decides to rescue a drug mule in this short story from the pen of G R Jordan.

Join G R Jordan's monthly newsletter about forthcoming releases and special writings for his tribe of avid readers and then receive your free Patrick Smythe short story.

Go to https://bit.ly/PatrickSmythe for your Patrick Smythe journey to start!

About the Author

GR Jordan is a self-published author who finally decided at forty that in order to have an enjoyable lifestyle, his creative beast within would have to be unleashed. His books mirror that conflict in life where acts of decency contend with self-promotion, goodness stares in horror at evil, and kindness blindsides us when we at our worst. Corrupting our world with his parade of wondrous and horrific characters, he highlights everyday tensions with fresh eyes whilst taking his methodical, intelligent mainstays on a roller-coaster ride of dilemmas, all the while suffering the banter of their provocative sidekicks.

A graduate of Loughborough University where he masqueraded as a chemical engineer but ultimately played American football, Gary had worked at changing the shape of cereal flakes and pulled a pallet truck for a living. Watching vegetables freeze at -40'C was another career highlight and he was also one of the Scottish Highlands "blind" air traffic controllers.

These days he has graduated to answering a telephone to people in trouble before telephoning other people to sort it out.

Having flirted with most places in the UK, he is now based in the Isle of Lewis in Scotland where his free time is spent between raising a young family with his wife, writing, figuring out how to work a loom and caring for a small flock of chickens. Luckily, his writing is influenced by his varied work and life experience as the chickens have not been the poetical inspiration he had hoped for!

You can connect with me on:
- https://grjordan.com
- https://facebook.com/carpetlessleprechaun

Subscribe to my newsletter:
- https://bit.ly/PatrickSmythe

Also by G R Jordan

G R Jordan writes across multiple genres including crime, dark and action adventure fantasy, feel good fantasy, mystery thriller and horror fantasy. Below is a selection of his work. Whilst all books are available across online stores, signed copies are available at his personal shop.

Cinderella's Carriage (Highlands & Islands Detective Book 39)

https://grjordan.com/product/cinderellas-carriage

A collector's prized possession vanishes without a trace. One of six magical carriages, each housing a precious gem. Can DI Clarissa Urquhart recover the set before the last stroke of midnight?

When a rare, jewelled carriage is stolen from a prominent Highland collector, DI Clarissa Urquhart is thrust into a glittering world of high-stakes collecting and fairytale obsessions. As she investigates, more carriages from the set disappear. With the wealthy victims reluctant to share their secrets, and a thief who seems to vanish like magic, Clarissa must piece together the puzzle before the full set is lost forever. As the clock ticks and the carriages vanish one by one, Clarissa finds herself in a race against time. Can she unmask the cunning thief and recover the priceless collection, or will this case shatter her career like a fragile glass slipper?

In this modern fairytale, every jewel has a dark secret, and happily ever after comes with a price!

Kirsten Stewart Thrillers
https://grjordan.com/product/a-shot-at-democracy
A luxurious spa on the Isle of Harris becomes a hotbed of suspicion. The star therapist is found dead in a seaweed wrap. Can DI Hope McGrath unmask a killer hiding behind a façade of island tranquillity?

When the lead therapist of an exclusive wellness resort is discovered murdered, DI Hope McGrath must navigate a world of alternative therapies and hidden agendas. As the team delves deeper, they uncover dark secrets beneath the serene surface of this Hebridean retreat. With suspects ranging from jealous staff to troubled clients, can Hope restore balance and bring a killer to justice?

On this tranquil isle, some come to heal, others to hide their sins!

Jac's Revenge (A Jack Moonshine Thriller #1)

https://grjordan.com/product/jacs-revenge

An unexpected hit makes Debbie a widow. The attention of her man's killer spawns a brutal yet classy alter ego. But how far can you play the game before it takes over your life?

All her life, Debbie Parlor lived in her man's shadow, knowing his work was never truly honest. She turned her head from news stories and rumours. But when he was disposed of for his smile to placate a rival crime lord, Jac Moonshine was born. And when Debbie is paid compensation for her loss like her car was written off, Jac decides that enough is enough.

Get on board with this tongue-in-cheek revenge thriller that will make you question how far you would go to avenge a loved one, and how much you would enjoy it!

A Giant Killing (Siobhan Duffy Mysteries #1)

https://grjordan.com/product/a-giant-killing

A body lies on the Giant's boot. Discord, as the master of secrets has been found. Can former spy Siobhan Duffy find the killer before they execute her former colleagues?

When retired operative Siobhan Duffy sees the killing of her former master in the paper, her unease sends her down a path of discovery and fear. Aided by her young housekeeper and scruff of a gardener, Siobhan begins a quest to discover the reason for her spy boss' death and unravels a can of worms today's masters would rather keep closed. But in a world of secrets, the difference between revenge and simple, if brutal, housekeeping becomes the hardest truth to know.

The past is a child who never leaves home!